Off Schedule

ANDREA BUCK

Published by Dreamland Publishing

First edition: June 2021

Cover Design by 100Covers.com
Interior Design by FormattedBooks.com

ISBN 978-1-7776968-1-8
ISBN 978-1-7776968-0-1 (ebook)

CHAPTER One

Why Valentina moved to Vancouver from Rio, I will never understand. If I had grown up in a place where you ate lunch on a beach, and if my hips could handle lunch and a Brazilian two-piece, I wouldn't have gone anywhere, least of all to a country where people play pond hockey four months of the year. Other people, not me. When I was young, I had to, of course, being Canadian and all. But my hockey career got cut short when a stick knocked out my braces before my parents had fulfilled their three-year payment plan to Jacobs Creek Orthodontics. My father carried me to the van, feet still in skates, and my mother yelled at me all the way to the clinic.

"Coffee?" I sign to Valentina on my way to the kitchen.

She confirms with a blink of her Bambi lashes, and I catch an evil eye from a guy in a yellow soccer jersey, Júlio César, number twelve. Like most of the people who first walk into our language school, he hasn't made it past the reception desk, hypnotized by our Latin goddess and her perfect smile.

As I pass by, Valentina explains the terms of our English immersion program to him. He leans in on one elbow and runs the fingers of his other hand through his hair.

"Tell me more about this upcoming school trip."

"Long weekend in Seattle," she says. "You'll love it."

"Will you be going?"

"I'm not a teacher, and besides, you want to learn English, *não é*?"

He slides a credit card her way and signs on the line where her scarlet fingernail is pointing. Impossible to resist Miss Leblon 2008. I'd never heard of the place, but according to Valentina, Leblon is the beach where the real *Girl from Ipanema* was walking. "They just couldn't make the lyrics work," she claims. There'll never be a song about Jacobs Creek. The rhyme would be impossible, and poison ivy ate our beach.

The kitchen looks messy as always. I start the coffee maker and rinse a pile of used plates. Something brown and crusty, at least two days old. Just as I'm starting to attack it with a foamy scouring pad, my phone goes off. It's my neighbor Max, a freelance jazz musician.

"Is our building on fire?"

"What? No," he says, and I hear a guitar doodling in the back, then drums and the high-pitched reverb of a microphone. Max is usually at, or on his way to a soundcheck.

"Why are you calling me at work then?"

"I'm at work, too," he says, then yells at his buddies to turn down the amp. "Plus, it's kind of important."

"Important for me or for you?"

"For me. And you. A business proposal actually, kind of urgent."

I'm guessing his car won't start and he has an out-of-town gig.

"I can't give you a ride today."

"It's nothing like that. I've got a job for you, an adventure rather. Pays well, too."

That's what he said when he played at a jazz club three hours north of here when we had to stay overnight because of unforeseeable weather conditions. The jazz club turned out to be the banquet hall of the local legion, and the weather was unforeseeable because Max had looked at the sky from his kitchen window and called it the forecast.

"I don't want to be a stagehand. You've asked me that before. I have a job, and it requires me to get off the phone now."

"I thought your school's closing down?"

"For only a week, Max. We're closing for renovations. And I have plenty to do in that time."

"Wait, Paula, let me explain. It's a trip to California, all expenses paid."

"Text me, bye-bye."

When something sounds too good to be true, it often is. When it involves Max, it always is.

"Thanks for the coffee." Valentina spins a few rounds on her swiveling chair before she stops to face me. "Is Dan really flying in just to supervise the renovations?"

"That's what his email said."

Dan's our boss, a nice guy in his fifties whose wife left him for a screenwriting barista. He's off coffee now and presently contracted to set up a chain of language schools in Taiwan.

"Is his girlfriend coming along?" Valentina combs through her endless hair with one hand.

"I don't think so. He wants to camp at the school and spend the weekend with his kids. Amber-Joelle doesn't do sleepovers." I point at a pile of blankets and pillows heaped on a half-inflated air mattress, which didn't feel like air when I carried it halfway across town.

"No, that doesn't sound like her," Valentina says. "God knows what he sees in her."

She gets up and walks toward the improvised campsite in the corner. "Did you bring all that on your bike?" She steps on the pump with one of her three-inch heels and abandons it after two attempts. "I really hope our boss knows what a loyal assistant you are. Remember, as soon as I have my degree—"

"You're taking me with you, I know."

I first met Valentina when she came here as an international student, her only English phrase being, "I am Brazil." She is now fluent, and one year away from a degree in business management.

She click-clacks across the room and slides into her winter coat.

"I think Philip went a bit overboard with this." She tightens her belt and adjusts the massive ring on her left hand.

"You must be the first one of the newly engaged to complain about too big."

I'd be happy to have one of those on my finger. Not for the fiancée part, but for self-defense. That thing could break someone's nose with the brush of a hand.

"The left glove does not fit anymore, look."

It sounds like 'clove' and 'feet.' Brazilian is hands down the chocolate mousse of accents. I guess I could move to another country, too, charm the locals with a foreign accent.

"You are coming to our party tomorrow, no? Philip has some delicious friends." Coming from her contoured lips, a wrong adjective sounds adorable.

"And Paula, sneakers are not an option, even if they're black."

I roll my eyes, promise to dress up, and crawl back behind my desk. Parties can be so stressful. The pressure to smile, to be witty, to keep my teeth clear of lip gloss and basil, not to mention the pain of standing in high heels. I wish I could just relax.

"Are you sure you won't need my help?" Valentina asks as she heads for the door.

"Thanks, I'll be fine. Have a good night."

I lock the door behind her, finish yesterday's pizza straight from the fridge, and go back to work.

The cleaning crew is arriving for the night shift when I get my bike from the storage room. I pull up my hood and brace for the cold that waits on the other side of the glass door.

OFF SCHEDULE

Why does November always bring never-ending gloom? The rain, the darkness, and the bleak expression on people's faces makes it hard to believe that the sun will ever come back to our part of the world.

The twenty-minute ride in the Pacific storm feels like an hour. I'm exhausted from pedaling against the wind, zigzagging around double-parked cars and braking to avoid the occasional pedestrian who runs across the street under a fluttering umbrella. I lean the bike against a fire hydrant and search my soggy pockets for my keys.

"Hi Paula," a familiar voice says from behind. It's Max, in a drenched suit. "Do you need help?"

Without waiting for an answer, he grabs my bike and carries it up the five steps into our hallway. With one hand he unlocks the door and holds it open.

"Thanks." I shake out my hair like a wet dog as I follow him to the mailboxes. "You look formal, where did you play?"

"Rehearsal at the City Ballet. Not me, obviously, I was the accompanist. Can you believe that? Playing a Steinway in a roomful of dancers? You should have seen them stretch. It's like my favorite fantasy came true and I get paid for it."

I grab my mail. Three flyers and a reminder that the car insurance is up for renewal.

"What's your secret dream?" He throws a handful of fliers in the trash. "If someone paid you to do your favorite thing."

"I don't know, get new tires?"

"I mean *hot* dream, Paula."

"Then I'd have to say, lie on the couch and watch Jude Law in *The Holiday*. All night long."

"Wow, that is one hot dream indeed." He fake-yawns to make his point. "Your next boyfriend's a lucky guy."

"Jealous?"

Max and I have been neighbors ever since I moved into the building two years ago. He's a pianist. When I asked him what he plays, he said something like, "post-modern free jazz meets metal." They say he is one of the best. I wouldn't know, so I measure his success by his ability to afford a two-bedroom unit without a roommate.

"So, about that job. All it takes is a sense of adventure and three days of your time."

"Can we talk about it tomorrow? I need to get out of these wet clothes."

"Sure. Wouldn't it be great to catch a flight somewhere south? Winter sucks." Max speaks while he checks his phone. "Oh sorry." He turns to face me with a grin. "You still won't get on a plane, right?"

I shouldn't have told him about the time I almost went to Brazil. Last winter Valentina invited me to visit her in Rio and stay with her family. Even though the Uruguayan low-cost carrier had four scheduled stopovers, the price was too good to resist. I felt it would be a good investment for the money my grandmother had left me. My doctor recommended Xanax. "Half a pill when you get to the gate," she said. "It'll just take the edge off."

And it did. In fact, so much edge was taken off that I slept through the entire boarding process and woke up three hours later with a stiff neck, drooling on my carry-on. I was the last person left at gate three and Pluma flight 509 en route without me.

Who knows if I'll ever get to see South America? I'm still a nervous flyer, my liver's a slow metabolizer, and Pluma Transcontinental is out of business.

"Sweet," Max yells and stares at his phone in disbelief. "The opening act for Bjorn Soerenson broke his arm."

"Oh?"

"And guess who'll be playing at the Orpheum now, for Reykjavik's hottest free jazzer? This one and his magical fingers." He wiggles his hand in front of my face.

"Congratulations." I have no idea who Bjorn Soerenson is.

"This is going to be my year, Paula, I know it."

His enthusiasm outweighs the fact that today is the 17th of November, which leaves him exactly six weeks to make it his year.

"The gig's in five days. I'd better get on it." He keeps hitting the elevator button. "I can probably get you a backstage pass, Paula."

"Great." I try to sound cheerful, but I'd be happy to miss the Icelandic superstar. Valentina's find-me-a-boyfriend event, and one of Max's concerts is a lot for one week.

"Wait, would you like to come to a party with me tomorrow night?" I jump forward to keep the elevator door from closing. "You could tell me about that job."

"Sorry, I really need time to prep for this gig."

"Brazilian." I improvise. "They're all Brazilian."

He mumbles something to himself, but I can hear a reluctant "okay" before the door closes. I push my bicycle into the storage room and head for the staircase. Poor Max, I don't think Valentina has any Brazilian friends in Vancouver. May the memory of stretching ballerinas linger throughout his weekend.

I moved into this building two years ago, after the love of my life had left for Australia without me. To be fair, we wanted to start a new life there together—Julian's idea. He got so excited about the job offer that he literally jumped on the next flight. I didn't mind staying behind a little while longer. Julian found us a beach house near Sydney, and I emptied the Vancouver home we had shared for two years. A week before my flight he told me over Skype that he had met someone, and he needed to sort out his feelings. I threw my laptop against the kitchen wall and got a five-hundred-dollar credit toward future travel with Singapore Airlines.

I was lucky to find an apartment so fast, even if it is in a faceless building at the other end of town. Faceless, characterless, everything-less. I guess it fit my emotional state at the time. Max, whose place is one floor above mine, came down one night to preemptively apologize for a band rehearsal that may go well into the night. He had expected eighty-five-year-old Mrs. Poliszczuk to open the door and it took him a moment to process that she did not live here anymore. We chatted for a few minutes and he invited me to come to the concert they were rehearsing for.

It wasn't really the kind of music I could relate to. Apparently, one needs to "educate the ear" before one can appreciate what sounds like five guys playing as loud as they can for as long as they can without agreeing on a scale. The concert was a huge success. NOW Magazine called them one of the top five alternative free-jazz bands to look out for.

A week later Max took me to his favorite Indian restaurant, and we shared a bowl of Navratan Korma, also called Nine Gem Curry. Or nine-times-too-hot curry. I told him about an Englishman who'd had a heart attack while eating insanely spicy food. Max said, "It's an urban myth." I don't think so.

Even though I wasn't ready to date again, I agreed to join him for open mic night at a comedy club, and we've watched a few movies together. He's seen me with a mud mask on my face, and I've advised him on pick-up lines that never work. Max is my best male girlfriend.

CHAPTER
Two

By the time Max comes to pick me up, I've cleaned the kitchen, reorganized the fridge, looked too closely at my bank account, gotten frustrated and spent an hour on Instagram, gotten more frustrated, eaten a whole chocolate bar, felt self-loathing and panic regarding my financial reality, and finally translated five pages of medical records for the Quebec health authorities into French.

Max is in his usual stage outfit, black jeans and T-shirt. He likes to be ready to play anytime, ever since his trumpet player friend was out on a boat and got a last-minute call to play with Michael Bublé's band. He had his instrument in the car, but it was the surfer shorts that kept him from playing the gig of a lifetime.

"Wow, did you change your mind about us?" Max looks me up and down. "That's a hell of a dress."

I give him a nudge and lock the door behind us. Maybe it was the salsa playlist that made me reach for this outfit. Maybe it was the tiny bit of wine on an empty stomach.

"The raincoat ruins it, though," Max says while we wait for the elevator.

I like this coat. It's cozy with tons of pockets, which means I won't need a purse, and it tones down this black strapless number. Also, it's the only thing I picked out myself. Dress: hand-me-down from my cousin who got pregnant after she bought it at a GUESS outlet in Vegas. Ankle boots: bridesmaid outfit at a disco-themed wedding. Choker necklace: same wedding.

I hope that Max is parked close by, otherwise I just wasted an hour trying to make my hibernating hair look glamorous. The belching from the depths of the elevator shaft sounds like a bulldozer digesting our building. I usually don't trust it and take the stairs, but the platform boots kill that option.

"So, where are we going?" Max asks while hitting the down button again. "Your stretch pants friend with the shaved head, or the pale one with the pet gecko?"

"I told you ten times it was because she lost a bet. And Freya is just taking care of her brother's gecko. His landlord's really uptight."

We watch the elevator door stutter open, taking its sweet time.

"Do you think I only have crazy friends?"

"I *know* that you only have crazy friends. You told me yourself at the Irish Pub on Halloween."

Damn, I talk too much when I've had a drink. Max blocks the door with his arm and lets me enter first.

"Holy smokes, somebody got high in here," he says.

Great, now I'll smell like a pothead.

"Anyway, where are we going exactly?" he asks.

I fill him in as we make our way to the car. It's been a while since I was picked up at my door for a night out, and when he offers me his arm to help me down the curb, I'm actually looking forward to the party.

"Sorry, the passenger door's busted." Max points at his car. "You can get in on the driver's side or sit in the back." I choose option number one and drag myself across the stick shift as gracefully as my dress allows.

"About that thing I mentioned yesterday," Max says while he wipes the fogged-up windshield with his sleeve.

"The job offer I can't refuse?"

He nods and adjusts the back mirror.

"I've been working on this deal, long story really. The short version is I know this guy who knows a guy who knows the ex-wife of a guy who collects vintage instruments. All played by famous people. From what my buddy tells me, he collects anything really, cars, watches, blondes. Then the dumbass cheats on his wife, she finds out, starts selling his stuff and takes off with a drummer, the guy I know."

"Where did she find a drummer?"

"She didn't know what the instruments were worth, so she went to a jazz club, asked around, fell for my guy. He arranged the sales for her and when the pissed husband came home to find his memorabilia room swiped, they took off together. The drummer owed me for not showing up at a gig once, so he made sure I got the deal on the bass."

Max hits the dashboard to wake up the speedometer which dies every time we drive over a bump.

"An original Prescott double bass."

"Did they elope to a tropical island?"

"Newfoundland. He's always broke."

True love. It's so cold over there.

"Anyway, I found a guy in California. He's totally hot for the bass, and we'd planned on meeting in Lake Tahoe next week. But now I have this gig on Thursday. Care for a piece of gum?"

He unwraps a Double Bubble and starts chewing. We barely move ahead in the Saturday night traffic.

"He insists on having it hand delivered and he doesn't want to wait. You know what rich people are like. Now," he pauses as he pulls over to let an ambulance pass. "How would you feel about a little road trip, all expenses paid, and make a thousand bucks on top of it?"

"Like some kind of bass trafficker?"

"Yes. No. It's totally legit. Just think of it as a fun trip. You go there, deliver the bass, maybe take an extra day or two, come back a thousand bucks richer, and make a good friend very happy."

"Don't you have anybody else you can send? Maybe someone who actually plays an instrument?"

"My bassist can't leave the country. Child support issues or something. Also, you look more trustworthy at the border, with your big blue eyes and high school hair."

"Are you crazy? I'm not driving anything into the United States that requires me to look trustworthy. What is 'high school hair' anyway?"

"You know, the girls from *The Brady Bunch*? The straight, no-frills hairstyle?"

"You watched *The Brady Bunch*?"

"My sisters made me."

He was some sort of later-in-life baby and his sisters were in high school when he was born.

"So, what do you think?"

"No way."

I regret bringing him. We remain silent for two blocks.

"It's just that we want to avoid declaring it, you know. Paperwork, taxes, not my thing. You just go there, tell them you want to see the Oregon coast, do some shopping, I don't know. Nobody's going to hassle you, I promise. I've been down there many times, instruments in the trunk both ways, no problem."

"You do it then."

"Something new like learn Japanese, or something new as in lying to an immigration officer?"

"You've got to lighten up if you ever want to find your own Jude Law." He blows a bubble and hits the gas.

I am not in party mood anymore. And I will never tell him anything again, ever. Other than "turn right here," we don't talk until we get to the high-rise overlooking the yacht club, where Valentina lives with her fiancé.

Philip is well-built and attractive, just like the apartment. He definitely loves Valentina, as he lets her cover the coffee table with wooden pineapples, a present from her mother, and accessorize the couch with blindingly bright pillows, embroidered with toucans by her Aunt Fernanda.

"Paula, my friend, you look so beautiful." Valentina flies toward me in a cloud of perfume. To call her nude-colored dress skintight would be an understatement. With her endless legs and smooth movements, she reminds me of a deer. If a deer had five-inch heels and hair down to the waist.

"This is Max."

I pull him forward by the sleeve. He has practically turned into a pillar of salt.

"Ah, you're the neighbor. So nice to meet you, please come in."

"He's cute, Paula," she whispers as we make our way to the living room. "Why are you guys not dating?"

I turn around and see Max behind us, gaping at Valentina's Samba walk. I stop and snap my fingers in his face.

"Stop staring, she's engaged."

He can barely form a sentence. "Did you see her? I mean … Can you learn how to walk like that?"

"Brazilian, I told you."

I'm still mad at him for suggesting that stupid bass mule job.

The music is Café del Mar, the food's color scheme matches the artwork. The room is packed with people in black, but I doubt they'll be performing at the Jazz Cellar after the party. Max scans the crowd looking for more Latin hotness.

"I'll get us a drink. What would you like?" he offers, probably glad for a reason to escape my frosty face.

"Pineapple juice, no ice."

As I am standing there, not sure where I belong, a voice so familiar I would have recognized it from across the ocean, pulls the ground out from underneath my feet.

"Paula Madeleine Murray, do you always ignore old friends?"

Everything starts shifting into slow motion and I am unable to move. My stomach is fluttering, my knees feel wobbly. I hold on to my purse like a lifeline and look for a place to sit.

"You look like a million. How are you?"

"Hi. Julian." The words get stuck in my throat, followed by a half-cough.

We kiss each other on the cheek.

I can't believe he's back and right here in front of me. The love of my old life, Julian. Sweet, smooth, painfully good-looking, makes-my-heart-ache Julian. Still the same cologne. I've always loved the combination of his warm skin and a hint of Calvin Klein Eternity.

When he pulls me close I almost faint. Valentina must have been in on the whole thing. He must have contacted her, they hatched a plan, organized this party, and here we are.

"Let's go, I found my coat." A high-pitched Australian accent cuts through the air.

I slide out of his arms and back into my senses. A six-foot blonde in glossy leggings is tapping on his back. She wears a see-through blouse and a bored look.

"Paula, Yvette. Yvette, Paula."

Soft handshake and an eye roll.

"Can we go now? I still have so much to do."

Like what, buy a bra?

"Just a second, angel, this is Paula, the girl I told you about."

How did he just introduce me? We lived together. I sat by his mother's bed at the hospital, and even hung up the nightmare of a painting she gave us for Christmas. In the laundry room, but still. Anybody who puts up with a crying clown above the dryer deserves more than, "the girl I told you about." The mention of my name seems to have no relevance to "angel" who proceeds to examine her hair for split ends. I want to scream.

"We're getting married the day before Christmas. Yvette planned the whole event all by herself. Maui, Lahaina Beach at sunset. It'll just be us and the family."

She briefly looks up when she hears her name. I bet she booked a wedding package online and called it event planning. Men are so stupid.

"We came back six weeks ago," Julian goes on. "The company needs me here now. They moved to the waterfront, my office has big windows. But this weather. I forgot how damp it is this time of the year."

And I forgot how he overtalks when he's nervous.

"What happened to 'marriage is so mainstream, it kills the romance'?" I ask, working hard to squeeze out a smile.

And what happened to playing it cool? I don't want to be the bitter ex.

"Well, you know, go with the flow is my new motto. Change is the only constant."

Reciting from some quote-a-day calendar is so not Julian. And a destination wedding? His mother will complain about the heat, the food, and all her imaginary ailments. Serves them right. Let Yvette-The-Wonderful deal with the hypochondriac cow.

Max is back with two glasses, heaven-sent.

"Here's your juice." He holds it out. "Pineapple, no ice."

I reach over and take the other one out of his hand.

"To new friends," I say, and take a sip of the drink Max got for himself. It tastes awful. I forgot he's into whiskey now.

Both men look at me as if I have two heads.

"You drink?" Julian asks.

"I thought you'd drive home." Max looks disappointed.

"Well, there you go, people change."

I finish the rest and introduce everybody.

"So, you're Australian?" I ask Julian's future wife.

Stupid question since her accent is thicker than her makeup. She gifts me with a nano nod.

"That's why we're getting married so soon. Yvette needs a work permit." Julian says, but then adds something with, "so in love …" when he catches her nasty glare.

I picture them on a Hawaiian beach at sunset, Julian in a tux, saying, "I do" to this creature in a wedding dress. As he lifts her veil, she has the face of a shark.

"What's new with you? Still working at the language school?"

"Yes Paula, what *is* new?" Max stares at me and sips lukewarm juice through a straw.

"No, that job, you know …" I try to figure out where to go from here. The whole room seems to wait in silence. "Just a temporary thing. Nine to five, same routine, blah blah. I'm my own boss now."

Did I really say that out loud? Judging by their looks, yes.

"You're freelancing?" Julian sounds impressed.

"Uh-huh." I lie.

That was easy. Paula is free. Lancing. What does it even mean? I look around the room and start feeling lighter. I should get business cards.

"You want to dance, sweetheart?" I blow a kiss toward Max and fake-smile until it hurts.

He looks confused as I push him toward the middle of the room where a couple of people have started to dance. The monotonous beat of Ibiza chill matches my mind. Everything's fine. Just a little white lie. Was it even? I could be self-employed. In fact, I am self-employed this week with the week off, unpaid, and the translation. Max hasn't moved yet, so I coil myself seductively into his body. He looks more frightened than aroused.

"You're my pretend boyfriend," I hiss and wave at Julian and his idiot fiancée. "Would you please play along until they leave?"

"And why would I do that?"

"Because we're friends, and friends help one another." I pull him closer and take the lead.

His hand starts gliding down my back.

"Pretend, Max. Pretend."

"Passion runs in my family," he says, "I'm one quarter Greek."

"I thought your folks came on the Mayflower."

"Some did, but Grandma was born in Crete."

Julian is watching us from across the room.

"Besides, you lure me here on a false pretext. No Latin babes except for the hostess, who is very much engaged. You've ignored me all night, made me lie for you, and now you don't like how I express fake love?"

He stops dancing.

"I'm sorry, Max. Just this one favor, pleeease. I promise I'll make it up to you." I rest my cheek on his.

The next tune is upbeat and tropical.

"May I lead now?" He squeezes me tight as our locked hips sway across the room. "Who is this guy anyway?" he asks and spins me around. "Don't tell me he's the reason you bought a new laptop?"

I almost trip, but he catches me.

"I thought I'd never see him again."

He pulls me into a close embrace.

"Your hair's so soft."

"You're a good dancer."

When the song is over, I head for the door, but Max grabs my hand and takes me back to the other end of the room. I feel Julian's eyes on me, but I try to ignore him.

"I think we need more drinks," Max says. "What can I get you guys?"

"I want to go home," Yvette says.

"Me too." The only thing we have in common.

Why are they still here anyway? The Outback bimbo has no interest in socializing. She leans against the wall and studies her nails. Sharp, shiny claws. I wonder if Julian's back is all scratched up.

"Here you are, sweetheart." Max is back and hands me a glass.

"So, what are you the boss of?" Julian asks and looks me straight in the eye.

I see a hint of familiarity, that warm spot which was my comfort and harbor for three years and eight months. He tilts his head and smiles almost invisibly. I cannot lie to Julian. He knows me too well.

"Well, the truth is." I take a big breath. "Actually—"

"The truth is," Max says and puts his arm around me. "That this woman, my amazing girlfriend, runs her own specialty courier company."

"Really?" Julian wrinkles his face in disbelief.

"What specialties?" Yvette's voice has the pitch of a smoke detector.

"Did you ever have to ship something that was too precious for the mail, like antique furniture or instruments, for example?" Max chirps.

"I use FedEx," squeaks the bitch.

"I mean really precious, something you don't want the FedEx guy to handle, even if he's Tom Hanks?" He gets more excited.

Yvette shrugs and goes back to what she is really good at: looking bored.

"And that's when you call," Max plays an air drum roll, "Deals without Borders, my girlfriend's very own company." He hits me between the shoulder blades like an Italian soccer player.

"Wow, Paula, that's fantastic," Julian says. "What a great idea, congratulations."

Our eyes lock and for a second I'm sure he feels what I still feel in the depth of my heart.

"As I've always said, anything's possible once you work through your fears." He swirls his glass until the clinking ice cubes sound like applause.

He keeps on talking, but I don't hear the words. My throat feels tight and I can't get enough air. Asshole. Arrogant supersized asshole. Who does he think he is, some freaking life coach?

I want to yell at him that he should go to hell with his stupid Yvette and their stupid Lahaina Beach or whatever it's called, and that they deserve each other, the cheater and the anorexic monster, and I never want to see him again, ever. And if this was a movie, or I was someone else, I would throw my drink in his face, because that's what I feel like doing, and I never had the chance to yell at him after we broke up.

But I can't. Because cool women don't do that. And I am cool. Why else would a professional pianist with great hair go out with me on a Saturday night? Also, I'm afraid that I might start to cry, and that would definitely not be cool.

And so, I take a sip of the drink, which is just as painful as the one before, and I make a promise to my anger that I'll let it out some other day. Tomorrow maybe. Or the next time at the laundromat when this uptight woman comes in just to wash her horse blankets. Who does that? Her husband's allergic to horses, she says. Go play golf or get a second washing machine. Last week I had to spend half an hour with a lint roller trying to get the horsehair off my sheets. What's that breathing exercise again? In with anger, out with love. In with anger, out with love. Exhale. In with anger. Another sip. I feel warm and slightly dizzy.

"So, Julian, everything's good. Really, really good. What am I saying? Fantastic. And you know what else is good? That I have Max and that my next job takes me to California. Did you know that? I'm going to Lake Tahoe. Have you ever been to Lake Tahoe?"

The room is spinning, and I hold on to Max's sleeve.

"We should really be on our way, sweetie. You've got quite the drive ahead of you." Max takes my hand.

"Let's all go out for dinner when you get back," Julian says cheerfully. Then he lowers his voice and leans in closer. "I forgot how cute you are when you're drunk."

Max wraps his jacket around me and pushes me toward the door. I don't see Valentina anywhere. Will call her tomorrow and explain.

"Hey guys, wait a minute." Julian follows us through the dancing crowd. "Why don't you both come to our place in two weeks? I'm having a Welcome to Canada party for Yvette. Here's my number."

"Thanks, man," Max says and puts the card in his pocket. "We'll see what we can do."

"What a jerk." I shiver as we march toward the car.

"Great party." Max dances around me and opens the driver's door.

I throw my shoes in the back and start crawling into the passenger seat. "You should really get that fixed."

As I drag my leg across the handbrake, the dress gets caught and rips apart at the seam. What the hell, it wasn't my style anyway. What I want to know is, what was my ex-fiancé doing at Valentina's, and why did I tell all those lies? I'm nauseated, and I want to go to bed.

"Shh, it's all good, have a little rest."

I open my eyes and see Max coming from the bathroom. He puts a glass of water on my bedside table and heads for the door.

"Do you need anything else? I've got to go." He looks at his phone and back at me. "See you in the morning, say around nine?"

"Max?"

He turns around, suppressing a yawn.

"That was really sweet of you tonight. Thank you."

CHAPTER Three

An earsplitting bang wakes me from the deepest sleep. It sounds like a wrecking ball. Does nobody care for weekends anymore? The chandelier in my bedroom sways dangerously from side to side. I jump up in an attempt to steady it and land beside the bed with a bang. Skin tingling, nose throbbing, it takes a second for me to realize what has happened. Instead of wearing my Snoopy pajamas, I'm in last night's dress, ripped open from the waist down. My knee hurts and blood's dripping from my nose. I get up in slow motion and limp to the bathroom.

Staring back at me from the mirror is a *KISS* impersonator whose makeup was done in the dark. How much did I drink? I peel off the remaining piece of fabric and step into the shower. Nothing, not even a drop from the creaking faucet. Is everything going wrong today? I grab a bottle from my gym bag and start rubbing French spring water on last night's makeup and today's nosebleed.

"Do you know what time it is?" I grumble as I open the door for Max.

"And a very good morning to you, too." He follows me to the kitchen. "Woah, somebody's in a bad mood. Good thing I brought some hot happy coffee."

He sets two paper cups on the counter and slides a brown bag my way.

"Geez, your place is tidy. If there's a kitchen table to have sex on, it'd be yours."

"Good one."

"The right guy might be just around the corner. Or on the floor above." He rolls up his sleeve and points at his flexed biceps. "Life's too short to be alone."

"I'll get a cat." I lift the lid of the coffee cup.

"You're too young. In ten years, maybe."

It's so annoying how everybody has an opinion about my life. Be more outgoing, use more makeup, find a boyfriend. I want to go back to bed.

"Why are you so cheerful this morning? Didn't you wake up from the hammering? I don't even have water."

"Nobody has water, Paula. They mentioned that on the note."

I stare at him and try to process what he's talking about.

"You know, the blue note that we all got in the mailbox?"

I might have used it to wipe gum off my shoe.

"They're turning the two top floor apartments into a penthouse. No water until four p.m., and construction noise till May."

"But it's Sunday."

Max bites into a muffin and looks like his usual happy self.

"Who cares?" He hands me a croissant. "You'll be gone for most of the week anyway."

"Where am I going?"

"The big adventure, being your own boss and all. You're driving to Lake Tahoe."

"No, no, no. That was part of the game, it wasn't real."

"Yes, it was," he sings and beams at me. "I pimped you up in front of that guy, swirled you around the dance floor, gave the performance of my life as your boyfriend, and you said you'd help me out. Or, as you put it, 'I will make it up to you, Max'."

I wish I could erase last night from my memory.

"Oh, if only there was something you could do to escape the noise," Max says with mock empathy.

As if on cue, somebody starts drilling upstairs. I sink into the couch and dunk the croissant in my coffee.

"That habit of yours makes you look old." He points at the drowned pastry in my cup. "As if you're toothless or something."

"That's how the French do it. And they have teeth."

"So, you *are* a world traveler?"

"I've got a translating job, twenty-five pages by Friday."

"This one pays better."

"My trunk's too small."

"Take my car."

"I'm running out of excuses."

Max high fives me with a grin.

I get up for more coffee. "And it's nothing illegal?"

He puts his hand on his heart. "My word."

I regret my decision the minute Max shows me the route on Google Maps. The thought of crossing the US border and driving up and down all those mountain passes by myself is too much at nine-thirty in the morning.

"What if I get stuck in the snow? Will there even be cell reception?"

"You're a Canuck, not a wuss."

"I've heard they detain people at the border for no reason, just because they have the same name as a terrorist suspect or something."

"Paula Murray?" He snorts. "Who would that be?"

"A Scottish separatist, trained by the Irish."

"Really?"

I nod and try to keep a straight face.

"Britain's so messed up," he says and shakes his head. "I'll come and get you if that happens, I promise."

"Thank you."

I fish a piece of croissant from my coffee. "Scottish separatist, really? You bought that?"

"What do you mean?" He looks up from his phone. "They do shit like that over there."

"No, they don't."

"They drive stick shift on the wrong side of the road."

It's beyond me how Max can link that to domestic terrorism.

"Now, when you get to the hotel, ask for Troy Beckett. I'll write it down for you." He scribbles the name on the Starbucks bag. "He'll be there until Wednesday morning, which gives you plenty of time to get to Tahoe and back by the end of the week."

"Will he give me cash?"

"E-transfer. Just call me before you hand the bass over and I'll make sure the money is in. So, you want to trade cars for the week?"

I have this mental image of me and the bass waiting by the side of the road while a merciful mechanic tries to locate a timing belt for his ancient Wagoneer.

"I've got another idea, maybe I won't need your car."

"Whatever, I'll fill it up anyway."

I get up and close the window. "Didn't I have a coat last night?"

"That thing from the KGB spyware store? Must have left it behind when you ran from your past."

My father is hosing down his pickup truck when I turn into our driveway.

"Paula." He drops everything and comes to hug me. "Did you fly out here? We only just hung up the phone."

"Three hours, seven minutes, Dad. My all-time record."

"This work project must mean a lot to you, driving all the way out here on your day off."

"Well, it's kind of a long story. I'll tell you everything when I get back."

We start walking toward the shed.

"Have you been sneaking a cigarette again?" I lean over and smell his sweater.

"Don't tell your mother. There's nothing else to do around here."

He has a point. Jacobs Creek, the town where I was born and raised, doesn't have a lot to offer, except for the highway to Vancouver. We never used it much, nobody did. "Why drive for a day, when you can order everything from Sears?" my mother would say. Going to the city was a big event in my family and we'd only do it for weddings or funerals.

Two other kids from my graduating class left Jacobs Creek. One joined the military, the other one's gay. Everybody else has moved to the next beige house and eats dinner at five.

"I didn't have time to fix the radio," my father says. "There seems to be a loose connection. It works sometimes, but don't rely on it. Everything else is as good as new."

We walk around the house and there it is, his pride and joy, a 1981 Winnebago Brave, beige with orange stripes. The colors have faded over the years, and the shape makes it look dated. I wasn't even born when it was built.

"How much do I owe you for insurance?"

"Pay me when you get back. All the paperwork is on the dinette."

"Thanks for doing that, Dad. I'll take good care of your baby, I promise."

"Are you sure you want to go across the mountains this time of the year? It can get pretty icy. You won't be able to use the water tank, either." He polishes the door handle with his sleeve. "Your mother doesn't like the idea of you driving this old thing one bit."

My mother doesn't like the Winnebago, period.

"I'll be fine." I try to convince both of us. "What can possibly go wrong with one of your vehicles?"

"I guess that's true." He adjusts his baseball hat and hands me the keys. "She's always been good to us."

My father loves this motorhome like family. For my mother it's a rather annoying in-law. He bought it when he was twenty-eight, with the intent of driving the Pan-American Highway to Costa Rica. Then he fell in love, got married, and my brother was born. They spent the wedding night at the hospital as my mother's water broke before they cut the cake.

We used to take it out on the road every summer, even after my brother and I had outgrown the age when camping with our parents was fun. Following my father's motto, "You never know what happens next," we had to get behind the steering wheel as soon as we could reach the pedals. I still don't know what circumstances could possibly require a twelve-year old to drive a recreational vehicle. My mother sat it out in the passenger seat until the road trip was over and she could get back to reading her romance novels.

"I'll quickly talk to Mom and then we can go over everything, okay?"

An hour later I'm back on the road, cautiously navigating each corner. After the side mirror hits a street sign on the first right turn, I make sure to swing out extra wide for the next one. The cupcakes my mother gave me for the trip tomorrow are delicious. If I keep eating at this rate, they won't even last a day. As she was taking them from the oven, she mentioned the Christmas card Julian had sent them.

"Julian writes you for Christmas? My Julian?"

"Oh yes," she said. "Birthdays, too. I always thought he was a good kid. Who knows, you two might still end up together."

I didn't tell her that the good kid is getting married in five weeks.

The engine howls as I merge onto the highway and I wave thanks to the truck driver who lets me squeeze in. There's a new-felt connection with everyone who sits up six feet high in the slow lane. We're like a family of elephants crawling uphill in one line. Two skimpy wipers fight against the deluge on the windshield, while the dashboard shows just the bare necessities.

It feels strange to be in the captain's chair. I should be back there with my brother, fighting over cookies or who gets to sit by the window. The carpet smells the same, a little bit musty and a lot like the inside of a thrift store. Years of family fun and leaking sinks. I feel lighter with every mile I leave behind.

People who would just drive through Jacobs Creek used to say how lucky I was to have grown up in such a scenic place. "So close to the mountains," they would say. "Gotta love the mountains." They didn't know that the mountains ate the sun every afternoon, that most things were gray, unless covered by snow, and that I only saw people from outside of our town when they stopped to fill up with gas. For most of my teen years I felt like a trapped raccoon dreaming of chewing its way to freedom. The day I graduated I got on the Greyhound to Vancouver.

I wonder how much of my old life I left behind, and which part follows me around as inevitably as shoe size nine. The first year on my own, I felt like I had Small Town Girl branded on my forehead. Lately it has shrunk to the size of an ankle tattoo. Most of the time anyway.

One night during the post-Julian-self-pity phase, after three hours of John Mayer's compilation album and some white wine, there was this sudden flash, almost a feeling of relief that I wouldn't have to move to Australia. I loved Julian more than anything. Couldn't we have had the perfect life right here?

The traffic is getting denser as I approach the city limits. My short trip to the past makes me appreciate the congested streets, even when I have to circle the block five times to find a parking spot near my apartment building. Eventually a Paolo's Pizza van takes off and leaves a spot just big enough for me to pull into. Funny, I still know the phone number of our favorite pizza place. Julian would always give me the mushrooms from his Quattro Stagioni even though he loved them.

CHAPTER Four

It's getting light when I carry my backpack downstairs. Clean linen and towels are always stowed under the bed and there's a five-gallon water container in the shower enclosure. I find enough cereal, crackers, and instant coffee to get me to Mexico. The motorhome hasn't been on the road in years, but I think my father sleeps in it sometimes. That's as close as he gets to living his dream.

Max crosses the street, embracing the bass like a friend after a pub crawl. Unshaven and in baggy pajama pants, he looks as if he's had a short night.

"Just put it on the bed in the back." I start the motor to get some heat. "Anything I need to know about the habitat of a double bass? Do's and don'ts?"

"Nah, just common sense. You'll be fine." He comes back to the front, gliding both hands across the plush sofa. "Wow, flashback to the eighties. Where did you get this beauty?"

"My parents' beach house, I told you."

At least the green velour says ocean. Faded, though, and a little murky.

"This would make the perfect tour bus. I should talk to your dad. Anyway, here's the address of the casino resort in Tahoe. My guy will meet you there on Tuesday at noon. And here's the money."

He counts ten one-hundred-dollar bills into my hand. "This is for your trouble, and this here," he holds out another five hundred, "is your expense account."

"Thanks." I put a couple of bills in my pocket and stuff the rest into a coffee jar.

"Hey, it won't hurt you to look a little bit more enthused. This is good money. Especially with them raising the rent and stuff."

"Raising the rent? How come I don't know about that?"

"I ran into the property manager last night."

"How did you run into her? I thought she only hangs out in her fancy harbor front buildings, as she never fails to point out."

"At the ATM," he says. "And then at Earl's." Barely audible.

"Excuse me?"

"She's really hot. And she gave me that look, you know?"

"What look? The I-can't-believe-how-simple-folks-live look?"

"Beats your judgy look."

"I'm not judgmental, just concerned."

"We had a couple of drinks, no big deal."

"That's all?"

He nods.

"About a hundred a month more, she said."

I'm one rent raise away from moving into some "centrally located bachelor pad," meaning a damp basement by the train tracks.

"I'll always have a spare bedroom for you, just roommates."

Gotta love Max for this.

"Anyway, I'm on a roll this week. First the concert, and now this deal. The guy already transferred a couple of grand last week. It's the easiest money I've ever made."

I wonder how easy it's really going to be. What if he just takes off with the bass?

"And don't worry. I've never met Troy, but he's a friend of a friend. Totally trustworthy."

"That's comforting." I don't think he hears the sarcasm.

"And Paula, use common sense. No hitchhikers, no deserted rest stops, you'll be fine."

We hug goodbye and Max starts walking away. His blue pants flutter in the wind like the Greek flag.

"Max." I lean my head out the door. "Will you come to Julian's party with me next week?"

He holds one thumb up without turning around. I lock the door and get in the driver's seat. A second later his head pops up beside the window and startles me.

"You want him back, don't you?"

It's almost dark and one yawn's following the next. Except for the three-hour border wait behind Tai Pan's Luxury Coach, everything's gone smoothly. My answer to the officer's question, "What's the purpose of your trip?" was plausible and almost true. I do intend to visit the Oregon Coast on my way back.

For now, however, there is nothing to do but drive. At times the miles fly by and I'm surprised to see the Seattle express lanes already, and then again, I'm moving at a donkey's pace.

The entertainment unit comes with three cassette tapes. Elton John, Frankie Valli, and The Carpenter's Greatest Hits. My parents were always a decade or two behind when it came to music. Our home was filled with the hits of the seventies, and when I was in junior high, I learned that ABBA had broken up years ago. My mother lives in denial.

I hang on to the radio station until the white noise swallows the faintest whisper of the radio host. Driving with nothing but the thoughts in my head gets annoying and I insert one of the tapes. Maybe it's the vintage vibe of the RV, or maybe I don't have to rebel against everything my parents like, but the music doesn't sound half as bad as I remember it.

"*Who loves you, pretty baby.*" I cross the Willamette River in Portland and sing along.

So eighties, and yet so romantic. To be the girl someone writes a song about. I thought I was lucky with a Hallmark card for Valentines.

I leave the highway somewhere past Salem and pull onto the parking lot of a generic mall. Home Depot, Michaels, Target, the usual. There's enough hot water left in the thermos for an instant coffee, and I need a break.

People roll out of their cars as if on autopilot. Screaming kids hang on to shopping carts, their parents too tired to care. A crow waits patiently for the crumbs the kid drops from her Happy Meal. I'll never admit it to Max, but I was secretly hoping that this would feel more like an adventure. I'm almost bored.

"*Because I'm happy*," Pharrell Williams sings from my cell phone. Unknown caller.

"Hi, Paula? It's Dan. Do you have time or am I interrupting something?"

He's always so polite, like someone from a different era. I wonder how he's lasted so long in the business world.

"I'm good, don't worry. How's your family? Are you enjoying the time with your kids?"

"Yes, wonderful, thanks." Muffled coughing. "Excuse me, I caught a cold on the plane. The flight was exceptionally long this time, or so it seemed."

This was almost Dan's word count for a day. He's not big on small talk.

"The reason I'm calling is, well actually, to thank you for finding me a mattress. Of course, you did a wonderful job preparing everything. And also, could you meet me for lunch tomorrow?"

"Would love to, Dan, but I'm out of town. Out of the country, to be exact. I'll be back in a few days."

"Well, that would be, I don't know. Where are you?"

"Halfway through Oregon, it's a long story."

"I see, that wouldn't work then. It doesn't matter, we'll find some other time."

Talking in fragments isn't unusual for him, but his mind seems more scattered than usual. Jetlag, I guess.

"Also, I left my Canadian phone at home, just brought the Taiwanese one, which is of no use here. You can get hold of me through the school phone, or at the Comfort Inn, room 314. They've started drywalling the office, it's too dusty to sleep there."

"Is there anything I can do from here?"

"No, no, don't worry. Just let me know when you're back." He hesitates. "The thing is, no, you know what, let's just meet on the weekend."

I'm back behind the wheel and drive for another two hours, then follow the signs to a commercial campground. Whispering Pines is a treeless gravel lot beside the highway. Other than the occasional high beams of a passing car, it's pitch dark. Once my eyes get used to it, I make out the shape of a large trailer at the other end. The campsite host, I assume.

I close all the curtains and double-check the door. Nobody knows that I'm in here, all by myself. There's no reason to be afraid, it's just like being at home. Except by the side of the road. With no neighbors. I want to call somebody, but the little line in the left-hand corner of my phone says No Service.

It's too chilly to get undressed, so I move the bass on its side and crawl under the covers in my travel clothes. This isn't so bad. It's a bit like camping, when Julian and I went to the Gulf Islands that one summer. It was the coldest August on record, but it was incredibly romantic to be huddled together in the same sleeping bag.

Now I'm alone, of course, just me and a supersized guitar. Maybe I should put my headphones on and listen to some music. But then I couldn't hear if anyone was outside. Now I remember why I've stopped watching thrillers, especially those crazy European ones. I once saw a Franco-Belgian film with subtitles, and now I have this terrible fear of public washrooms. And Belgium.

The furnace fan kicks in every time the temperature goes below sixty. It starts with a bang and slowly turns into a low buzz. As soon as my ears have adjusted to the sounds inside, the outside becomes louder. An animal howls in the distance. Or is it a tuned-up car? The awning rattles at unpredictable intervals. Could be a raccoon. I reach under the bed. Good, the old baseball bat is still there. Tomorrow I'll find a more hospitable place to spend the night.

The next morning starts out gray, but it gets sunny once I reach the last stretch of the endless ups and downs of Grants Pass. I couldn't wait to break camp this morning. The light of day revealed that I was the only person at Whispering Pines. Even the campsite host had a sign on his fifth wheel, *Back in March.*

Max had recommended stopping in Mount Shasta, Muladhara Chakra of the world, he said. His ex-girlfriend moved there to be "close to the source."

"Don't contact her, though. Not the forgiving type. She'll hate you by association."

I take the exit for town center and pull into the first gas station. It's snowing lightly, and except for a white-haired man and his dog, nobody is outside on this Tuesday morning. It's only been one day of solitude, and half a day without radio, but with all the quiet time, a tiny bit of loneliness is tiptoeing around, and I don't want it to move in with me.

Shasta looks like a charming small town. A modest beauty, with its well-kept store fronts, Christmas lighting and smiling reindeer. I follow the arrow on a handwritten chalkboard that says All Day Breakfast At The Bear Café and slide in line behind an older couple.

The buttery smell of hot pancakes is inviting and beats the cereal bar I almost choked on this morning.

Every booth is taken, so I climb onto a bar stool by the coffee machine. So far, I'm not feeling anything, chakra-wise. The waitress knows everybody and is actively involved in at least three conversations simultaneously. While she compliments someone on her new haircut, and another patron on the birth of his tenth grandchild, she juggles the cash register, fills up coffee mugs, and takes orders. I go for a fruit cup and the special of the day, Cinnamon Roll French Toast. I need comfort food after the bad dreams at Whispering Pines.

Two women around my age sit at a table beside me. One is dressed in orange from head to toe and has a loud voice. The other one sits with her back toward me. All I can see is her curly head nodding continuously while the loud one's talking. Their table is so close that my leg gets tickled by the hood of her orange ski jacket.

"Then she touched my feet and oh my gosh, I saw this bright light, like you can't imagine. I mean so bright. Beaming. And suddenly it was my body down there and me hovering above my own life, and like, totally peaceful, you know, and I was like, why do I even worry, you know what I mean? Totally unreal. You gotta see her."

The curly one stirs her coffee vigorously.

"I don't know. With everything I tried, I should be feeling something by now. And the rebirthing was so expensive."

"What about the crystal pyramid?" the orange one interrupts. "You felt something there, didn't you?"

"Well, of course I felt something, the guy was insanely cute," she says and stirs a bit faster. "Do you think it means something that he follows me on Twitter?"

"Did you add him first?"

"Well, yeah."

The orange one scans the room.

"Could I borrow your ketchup for a sec?" she asks me.

"Sure." I hand her the bottle.

"You're Canadian?"

She got that from 'sure'? With a mouthful of cantaloupe, I nod.

"The key ring gives it away." She points at the red maple leaf next to my plate. "I love Ryan Gosling."

"I've never met him."

"Oh my gosh—I love your accent. What about Ryan Reynolds?"

"Haven't met him either."

How small does she think Canada is?

"Oh well, too bad. Do you know that your aura is beautiful? Totally balanced, lots of blue."

Of course, she would see lots of blue. That's pretty much the only color I'm wearing today.

"Thanks." I eat faster. At this point Belgian movies turn psycho. A harmless chitchat about keyrings, but what she really wants is Ryan Reynold's address or one of my kidneys.

The sun feels nice on my face as I walk around the block before heading back to the RV. The stores along Main Street offer everything from real estate to grounding, and since I haven't brought a single book on this trip, I go into a cute looking store named ReBook. The owner, or Co-Op, as I learn from the Welcome sign, must have a thing for seasonal decoration, as the doorway is overgrown with garlands and tinsel. I duck under strands of lights to get inside, where the sound of pouring rain reminds me of Vancouver Island. *Clearing the Mind - Rainforest Part I*, the CD cover by the till says.

I cautiously move around a life-sized Rudolph made out of papier-mâché when my ponytail gets stuck in his antlers and almost brings him down. Nobody sees it and I put everything back together. Hoping to find a light read for the trip, I look through all three aisles. Most books have titles like, *How to Want What You Have and then Give it All Away*, *Tantra for Tent Camping*, and *Barefoot: A Revolution.* I think I'm in the wrong place. A long-haired guy in a shirt that reads, I Like Turtles, asks me if I need help finding anything.

"Yes, thank you. I'm looking for the latest Grisham."

"The lawyer?" he asks.

I nod.

"We don't carry anything with negative energy."

"Oh, I see."

His mouth keeps smiling while his mind is non-judging me.

"How about something historical?" I ask.

"We believe that dwelling on the past gets in the way of living in the now."

"So, you don't have any?"

"No."

"Something humorous? Do you sell funny books?"

"Fiction?"

"That would be great."

"No."

I slowly walk back to the front wondering what could possibly be wrong with comedy, while the turtle shirt explains to me that fiction means denying what is, and humor can be offensive.

"Take this one, it's amazing," he says and grabs a book from a bin by the door. "Twenty-five percent of all proceeds go to the Peruvian rainforest."

He tilts his head and points up in the air. "Listen," he whispers. "Isn't it magical?"

"Not a big fan of rain, sorry."

He looks offended, so I pay four dollars for the book in his hand and leave the ReBook factory of enlightenment. Once outside, I look at the title of my purchase. *Never Alone—Messages from the Animal Kingdom* by Prakash Johnson. As I walk back to the parking lot, the animal kingdom sends its first message: Don't step in dog shit. Thank you, I knew that, but it looked like a leaf.

For my second night on the road, I go for a Walmart parking lot. Max told me that it's safe and legal, except in Portland and Boca

Raton. After the deadly silence of Whispering Pines, I feel comforted by the sounds of idling trucks and shopping carts being banged into each other.

I take shelter in the shadow of a spaceship-sized Endeavor XE. Generator on, antenna up, blinds down. A silver-haired couple in matching track suits step outside. They both have the waddling gait of those waiting for, or recovering from hip surgery. He starts to attack the windshield with a Windex bottle, while she carries the poodle to a grassy spot by the trash cans. The back of her jacket says Vitalife Consultant. I wonder what their dreams were when they were young.

I open a can of soup, Nature's Finest Harvest Bisque. The bisque looks like dish water and tastes even worse. I dump it all in the sink and go to bed hungry. There's barely a bar left on the phone battery, so I flip through my new book. "Each spirit animal has valuable information and meaning as it crosses the path of your life. Whether it is a hummingbird or a hawk, be still and ask yourself what it has to tell you." The letters on the page turn into dots and nothing makes sense anymore.

CHAPTER Five

The next morning starts out freezing cold and my cup of Folgers Instant tastes like heaven. I roll the bass back into driving position and secure it with pillows and blankets. It's still dark when we leave the world's biggest retail campsite.

After three hours of driving on Highway 5, which means each cassette played once, both sides, and then back to the first one, it's a welcome break to turn onto the mountain road into the Sierra Nevada. The air is colder up here, and the snowline closer. The Winnebago has proven to be a reliable travel mate and I feel bad for putting all that stress on a senior. My GPS is a fold-out map on the passenger seat which obviously won't inform me should I ever take a wrong turn. I turn off the radio. Karen Carpenter's voice has no chance against the roaring engine.

I turn left and follow the signs to the Nevada state line. After a couple of short glimpses, a large part of Lake Tahoe lies right before me, like a mirror in the sun. I pull onto the shoulder and turn off the motor.

How quiet it is. I open the window and take a deep breath. The view below me is a high-gloss brochure come to life, the water glistening, little white clouds reflected in the lake. The colors couldn't be more brilliant in July. I just sit and take in the deep blue and turquoise. The air is cool as it floats over my face and I smell pine trees. I've never been on a quest for bliss or happiness. Life happens, and some days are better than others. But this moment holds something special, a promise of peace that I wasn't even looking for.

The sound attack of a Heineken truck Jake-braking downhill reminds me that I'm here on business. I close the window and look at the clock. Eleven-forty. I'd better get going.

Oversize parking at the Diamond Mountain Resort & Casino is at the farthest end from the main entrance, halfway around the building. I lock everything and squeeze the bulky bass through the RV door, careful not to damage it on the last few steps of our journey. Just as I try to heave the thing onto my shoulder, a uniformed hotel employee walks toward me and points to the right.

"The stage entrance is over there," he shouts from the distance. "The rest of the band's already here."

Despite his inhospitable tone, I feel flattered to be taken for an artist.

"Thanks, but I'm not with the band."

"My apologies. Do you need a hand?"

The lobby is as empty as the parking lot. It's almost noon. At the front desk, I ask for Troy Beckett. The blonde receptionist slides her hair back, checks the computer screen, punches some keys, and shakes her head.

"We have no reservation under that name. Maybe you have the wrong hotel."

She doesn't even look at me. Size zero with an attitude.

"If I can just charge my phone for a minute, I'll give my friend a call."

She sighs and looks around, as if I'm asking the impossible in the middle of her busy day. Then she opens the latch of the little gate that separates the lobby from the staff. I suppose she'll show me to the business center.

I pick up the bass and follow America's Next Top Model across the lobby. She walks so effortlessly in her tight uniform, burgundy pant suit with matching pumps. Like a Porsche on a runway. *Click clack click clack*, her heels accelerate. It's hard to keep up with her. Drenched in sweat, lugging what seems like a hundred pounds of wood in a canvas bag, I feel like a thirty-year old pickup truck. I almost trip when the floor changes from tile to carpet. The front desk diva sways onto a multi-purpose mini stage, much like the one at the Jacobs Creek Ukrainian Church where we used to have choir practice.

"There." She points at a spot behind a fake palm tree. "Do you need anything else?"

I get on my knees and crawl to the vacuum cleaner outlets, careful not to get in the way of her stilettos.

"Thank you." I look up from the floor and try to read her nametag. "Belope."

Without a word she catwalks back to the front desk. Maybe it's pronounced, Belopé.

I prop the bass between two planters and plug in the phone. Then I lean against the wall and wait for my heartbeat to get back to human range. Note to myself, resume cardio workout.

Three missed calls from Max last night and two messages sent this morning. "Call me when you get this. Where are you? Need to talk."

None of this sounds good. He picks up after the first ring.

"Hey Paula, where are you?"

"Hotel lobby, just as you told me. But your guy isn't here."

"Yeah, that's what I was calling about. There's a small change of plans."

I don't like the sound of that.

"Troy had to leave on short notice. He says he's sorry."

Max sounds as matter-of-fact as an airport announcement, *American Airlines flight 509 has a gate change.*

"So, I'm driving straight back home with that thing?"

The whole trip for nothing, what a nuisance.

"Basically yes." Max clears his throat. "Except the bass won't be coming back. And you're taking a different route."

"Huh?"

"Troy's in Vegas now." His voice is turning into post-delay airline timbre, *we apologize for any inconvenience caused and hope to welcome you soon on one of our flights.*

"He wants you to meet him there the day after tomorrow. He'll be at the Paris for lunch."

I hope he's joking.

"Paula, you still there?"

"Uh-huh."

"What do you say, Las Vegas? Sit by the pool, try a few slots?"

"Are you kidding me?"

"I looked it up on a map, can't be more than eight hours from where you are now."

"I'm not going to Vegas."

"Look, I know it's a lot to ask, and you're right, it wasn't part of our deal. But I couldn't know the guy would take off like that. Please, is there any way you can help me?"

I slide down the wall and sit on my heels.

"I'll give you an extra five hundred bucks."

"That's not what we agreed upon, Max. How can I be back home in two days?"

"Eight hundred, plus expenses. Please."

I'm hungry and tired, my last shower was on Sunday and my self-esteem's not at its peak. I don't know if it's the fumes from the plastic plants, but when I squint my eyes the stains on the carpet look like snowflakes. Eight hundred dollars is a lot of money.

"Okay," I hear myself say. "Thursday, noon, lobby at the Paris."

We all have our price.

Belinda-Hope keeps a poker face when I ask for the room rates. With her hair cascading down the other breast, I can now read her full name.

"The mid-week special's ninety-nine. It comes with a ten-dollar voucher for the casino. The renovated rooms on the Privilege Floor have a lake view and—"

"The special please."

I hand her my credit card.

"There's a surcharge for early check-in."

They better have fluffy robes.

Half an hour later I have an overheated room on the fourth floor, a player's card in my name, and a hot bath in a shell-shaped tub with jets. The pink tiles make the room look dated. Like an old movie set for Elizabeth Taylor. I drink water from the beak of a golden swan and ignore my nagging cell phone in the other room.

CHAPTER Six

The evening news on the TV next door wakes me up from the deepest sleep. I'm spread out across the bed, and for a second I don't know where I am. The clingy thing wrapped around my thigh doesn't feel like the duvet at home. I roll over and fumble around until I find the bedside lamp. With the light on, I see it's the flesh-colored Vellux blanket, the one I'd carefully folded into the sheet before I crawled into bed. It sizzles and sparks as I kick it away.

In the daylight, the room didn't seem so bad. Now it feels oppressive. Everything's dark and dated, and I don't feel like getting up. Maybe there's a pizza menu in the drawer and I can stay in bed. No, just the Book of Mormon and We-Care-About-Your-Opinion cards. While my limbs sag back into the clothes I've worn for the past three days, I listen to the message on my phone.

"Hi Paula, Dan here, 250-438-7991. I know that we said we'd meet on the weekend, but maybe you can give me a call after all. Whenever it suits you, it's not urgent. But call me anyway. I need to discuss something. Oh, and it's Tuesday. Bye."

He still doesn't trust modern technology, as he refers to texting and caller ID, and always leaves detailed voicemails. I try to get hold of him, but he doesn't answer.

Even with its tired light bulb, the bathroom mirror is brutally honest. My face looks like a white canvas and I wish I'd packed some beauty utensils. At least my hair doesn't look too bad. It's tousled and wavy from sleeping on it after the bath. Julian once said I looked like a mermaid. We must have been freshly in love.

The hallway with its flaking wallpaper and intimate lighting has got its charm, like an aging movie star. The elevator doesn't. A mix of vomit and Lysol makes me hold my breath to the mezzanine floor. From here I have a good view of the gambling hall, which, although big, is anything but glamorous. More like a Walmart with chairs. I take the escalator down and move forward with the crowd. Where do all these people come from? Most of them are my grandparents' age and nobody's dressed like James Bond. Cigarette smoke hits me like a wall of fog and my first impulse is to run while I can still see the exit sign. Then again, all that awaits me upstairs are the Latter-Day Saints and cable.

While Sinatra doobedoo's from a ceiling speaker, I walk along the rows of slot machines. A cocktail waitress with hair too long to be real puts down her tray of empties and wipes around the cup holders at the Wheel of Fortune. I'm sure she'd rather be home reading to the grandkids.

"What can I get you, hon?" She tries to be cheerful, but her voice is tired.

"Vodka-orange would be great, thanks."

She doesn't say anything as she moves along, checking for full ashtrays on the slots. People around me stare at the screens without blinking, their drooping necks connected to the slot machines with coil lanyards. I can't tell if they're winning or losing, if they're happy or sad. Every once in a while, someone gets up and plugs the lifeline into another machine. Maybe that one will change everything.

"One screwdriver over here."

The waitress is back and hands me my drink. When a chair opens up at Noah's Arc, I seize the opportunity and put my Premier Players Card into the slot.

After pressing a few buttons, the little pictures start spinning around. Once they're settled I have a camel, two sheep, and a Noah. I start a new round. The electronic coin-rattle and the flashing lights tell me that something great is about to happen. Three Noahs line up—I just made five dollars.

The waitress comes with another drink. Cheers to my lucky night. I put three dollar bills on her tray and keep going. During the next half hour I lose one buck, make two, switch seats twice, and end up with the ten dollars I started with. I pull out my card and wander around. One last game, then I'm out of here. The hall is full of loneliness and heart disease. Portable oxygen tanks heel by their owners like faithful pets.

Someone's just gotten up from the Reels Royce. It accepts quarters only, but there's no other free spot. With all those pictures spinning, and Petula Clark screaming, *Downtown*, I regret my decision and wish I'd gone upstairs. The rattling and ringing become one in my head and it takes all my energy to focus on the screen. It's so hot in here. I try to stand up and sag right back into the seat. I take a deep breath when a wave of perfume rolls over me.

"Are you all right, dear?"

I turn around and see the powdered face of an elderly lady too close to mine. She smells like syrup and roses, and the scent competes with the smoke around. Her slender body is dressed in Capri pants and a blouse that looks as if it was dragged across a painter's palette. A halo of ringlets is held in place by a headband. Where I grew up, ladies her age kept their hair short and their wardrobe beige.

"Thanks, I'm fine. It's just the air."

I close my eyes and fan my face with a napkin. The perfume has hijacked my senses and I wish she would leave. I peek to the right and watch her settling in on the chair next to mine.

"Would you like a piece of orange?" she asks and holds out a freezer bag.

Her bright eyes look ageless despite the wrinkles that frame them.

I shake my head. "No, thanks."

She chews on the flesh of a sliced orange, puts the peel in the ashtray, and drops the Ziploc back into her oversized beach bag. I don't want to talk to crazy strangers, so I press some buttons on the Reels Royce and pretend to be playing.

"You have to insert the card, dear."

She looks at me with expectation. Now I see that all those dots on her blouse are parrots. Hundreds of little parrots, some in flight, others resting on palm leaves. Each time she moves it looks as if the fabric on her body has come to life.

"Maybe it's time for a change," she says and gets up. "You seem to be stuck here. Whenever I have one of those moments, the wolf puppies over there bring me luck."

It doesn't interest me one bit what the puppies do or don't do, or what 'one of these moments' even means, but seconds later I find myself pushing paw-shaped buttons while she waves the waitress over and orders a gin-tonic and, "whatever it is that she's drinking."

"Try ten lines this time," she says, her eyes twinkling.

I obey and get punished with a three-dollar loss.

"It didn't work. Now what?"

"Wait, let me try one round."

She bets the maximum for this machine and wins twenty dollars.

"Nice start," she says, and prints out the receipt.

Our drinks arrive, and the parrot lady raises her glass.

"Cheers, I'm Rita."

"Paula."

"Nice to meet you, Paula. Do you come here often?"

"It's my first time."

"Really? I'm here once a month, sometimes twice. Are you all by yourself?" She takes the decorative lemon slice from her drink and sucks on it. She's the only joyful looking person in here.

"I was meant to meet someone here, but it didn't work out. I'll be leaving tomorrow morning."

"Where are you going, Sacramento? Or the coast?"

So many questions, I wish she'd leave me alone.

"Vegas."

As if touched by an invisible current Rita sits up straight.

"You must be so excited, everybody loves Vegas."

She puts the lemon peel back in her glass and rubs her hands together.

"Actually, I'd rather get back home. I'm not a gambler."

Her smile vanishes for a second.

"Vegas is so much more than casinos. It's charming. It's lovely. If people only made an effort to look deeper."

I feel as if I insulted her favorite child.

"I'm sure it is. Anyway, I'd better keep going and find something to eat before the restaurant closes. I haven't had dinner yet. Nice talking to you."

Please, bird woman, fly away.

"They're open twenty-four hours. I can tell you're a rookie. Are you not eating this?" Her smile is back, and she points at the candied cherries dangling from my glass.

I pass it to her and get up. "Take care, Rita, and good luck for the rest of the night."

"Enjoy your trip and play one slot for me in Vegas, will you?" She pulls a couple of dollar bills from her bag and puts them in my hand.

"You don't have to give me money. I may not even have time for a casino visit."

I try to give the bills back, but she pulls her hand away.

"Keep them for good luck then."

The Lakeside Bar & Restaurant is on the lower floor and has no windows. If it wasn't for the painting of a lake, I could just as well be in Kansas. The place is surprisingly full for a weeknight and the hostess leads me to a table near the entrance. She takes away the extra placemats and picks up the cutlery that was set for a party of four.

The couple across from me watches every one of her movements, as if they're judging my singleness before they go back to slurping their soup.

I've just returned from my second trip to the buffet with a plate of tacos, when I see a canvas bag with white and yellow stripes waiting in line. Its owner is in an animated discussion with the hostess, who, from the looks of it, won't let her enter the restaurant. I quickly slide into the booth and lower my head. Not low enough, though, as Rita has made it through and found me in my singles booth.

"The hostess wanted to charge me for the full buffet. Can you believe that? Even though I kept telling her I was meeting someone just for coffee."

She smiles as if we're long-lost friends and slides into the seat across from me.

"So, how's the food? Do you feel better now?" She puts her bag on the seat beside her and orders a decaf.

I nod and try to make sense of the situation. Is this woman stalking me? Of course, I'm not scared of a senior, it's just weird. I look at the couple who were staring before, but they're too busy to notice that I have company now. The guy dropped his plate of meat and gravy and now they're shuffling back for another load.

Rita seems to be watching the entrance area, looking at her watch, and then back to the hostess. Eventually she directs her attention toward me.

"What are you having for dessert? The best part of the meal if you ask me."

She's so petite, I can't imagine that she eats dessert too often.

"I'll skip it. I ate way too much already."

Her eyes may have just lost some of their sparkle.

"Would you like something with your coffee?" I ask her. The full buffet's paid for anyway.

"How sweet of you. Do you think you could get me a chocolate éclair?" She beams like a child.

I come back with a plate of pastries and place it between us. Rita puts a small chocolate cream puff in her mouth, just as a waitress stops by our table. How petty, it's only dessert.

"Do you belong to the group from Yuba City?" she asks. "Your bus is boarded and ready to leave."

"Nobody at this table for Yuba," Rita says and licks her lips. "Try those folks over there."

"Sorry," the waitress says. "I just thought—"

Rita puts the empty breadbasket in her hand. "Thank you, dear, that would be all. Could we get some water when you have a chance?"

Rita folds her hands on the table.

"So, where were we? Oh yes, éclairs. The best ones I've ever had were at the Paris Hotel in Vegas. You should try them when you have a chance."

"Funny you mention that. It's exactly where I'm going."

"Small world."

She smiles and takes another bite. When she's done chewing, she leans forward.

"You know, it's just a thought, and you can say no, of course"—she dabs her mouth with the napkin and clears her throat—"but would it be possible for you to give me a ride?"

"I'm sorry, but I've had too much to drink tonight, I really can't drive."

"Oh no, I mean tomorrow. Would you please take me to Vegas?"

I want to shout *no* from the top of my lungs. I need my space, I have things planned, I don't want to talk, and we just met an hour ago. She looks at me like a caged dog, as if her whole life depends on the outcome of my decision. This is ridiculous, I don't have to say yes.

"I will pay you for your trouble, of course. We can split the gas. I won't be a bother."

I need an excuse, and I need it fast. Bulky load? Passenger seat broken? Funny how lying seems to be the easier option lately.

"I'm sorry if I overwhelmed you. I shouldn't have asked."

A waiter fills up our water. His name tag says Julian.

"You can come with me," I blurt out.

The young waiter looks scared.

"Not you, her," I say to him.

Rita claps her hands and smiles as if she's won the jackpot.

"You have no idea what that means to me. You just made me very happy, Paula. Thank you, thank you so much." She looks down at her watch and I can see that her roots haven't had a touch-up in a while.

"I can't drive you back here, though. Do you have a way to get home?"

"Oh sure, don't worry. Just drop me anywhere in Vegas. I'll find my way around. You won't even know I'm there."

"Okay then, Rita, I guess I should get some sleep now. I'd like to leave around eight. Do you live nearby?"

"Let's meet in the lobby. I don't want to trouble you any more than I already have."

"See you in the morning then. My room number is 1006, if you change your mind." I write it down on a napkin. "How can I reach you, just in case?"

"I'll be there."

CHAPTER Seven

I hit the snooze button so many times that there's no time for a shower. What a stupid idea to take the old lady along. I could just as well have stopped at the first gas station and picked up the hitchhiker with the cardboard sign Anywhere South.

For a split second I think about ditching her. Clearly, I wasn't thinking straight last night. Maybe they put something in the drinks to get people to spend more money at the slots. And then there was Julian's voice in my head, all judgmental, and how I'm always stuck in fear gear. I want to see his face when I tell him my story next week.

The bass bag gets caught in the door on my way out. It rips with a quiet sigh, right above the handle. Dammit, does everything have to go wrong on this trip? I open the zipper and check for scratches on the instrument. There are some, but if this thing was really built in the eighteen hundreds as Max said, how can one tell if it's from old age or a bang against the door? The brown bag doesn't look fancy and smells as if it's been rotting away in somebody's garage for the last hundred years.

A Breakfast-On-The-Go table is set up in the corner of the lobby. I'd love to take something for the road, but my hands are full. I fold the invoice into my pocket and see Rita walk out of the restaurant.

"You're really here?" She sounds almost surprised to see me. "Let me help you carry that. I had no idea you're a musician."

"I'm not, but that's another story. Would you mind getting me a muffin and some coffee from the free buffet?"

"With pleasure," she says and moves toward the buffet. Even in running shoes there's something elegant about the way she walks. She's probably a lovely lady.

I watch her fill two cups and grab a couple of yogurts. Then she waits until the concierge gets busy with a group of guests and empties all the baked goods into her bag. Unbelievable. Am I the only one who saw that?

"Shall we?" she asks and walks through the revolving door.

I look at the empty pastry tray and feel a strange sense of justice. Twenty bucks for early check-in is ridiculous.

The temperature has dropped considerably since yesterday and there's a thin layer of snow on the ground. I pull the collar of my coat tighter while Rita bounces beside me in another summery blouse from her cruise collection.

"Aren't you cold?" I ask as we cross the parking lot.

"We're going south, aren't we?"

Judging by her beach bag, we certainly are.

"This is it." I unlock the door and offer her my arm, but she jumps right up the steps.

"I'm so excited, this is even better than I thought." She climbs into the passenger seat and starts adjusting the backrest. "Why did you spend the night at the hotel when you have this?"

"The water tank's empty." I don't have to share my fear of deserted campsites with her.

"Would you like your breakfast now or later?"

She opens her bag just enough for me to see the assortment of buns, croissants, muffins and yogurts, some mandarin oranges, and two bananas. I take a buttery croissant and hope that she's not on California's Most Wanted list.

A good three hours into our journey and we haven't seen one gas station. While I've learned the milestones in Rita's life—born in Sacramento, widowed, Frank being the love of her life—she has a way of turning the conversation right back to me.

"Do you not miss being in love?"

"No. Well, maybe a little bit."

Her directness makes me uncomfortable.

"Did someone break your heart?"

She sure is persistent. With a sweet voice, though. Like hot chocolate on a cold day.

"Something like that."

"I see. Is this trip an escape then?"

"No, not at all. It's a job, kind of."

I hope the interrogation's over when she bites into her muffin.

"You can't run away from love," she says in between bites. "It doesn't work."

"I'm not. There's nothing to run away from."

"Why aren't you enjoying your trip then? I have the feeling your heart is a bit heavy."

"Are you a therapist?"

She laughs. "I'm not. But I've been around for a while, and I know a thing or two about love."

The moment at Valentina's party comes to my mind, and how Julian took me in his arms.

"I ran into someone last weekend, and it brought up memories, that's all." The gentle kiss before I left. "And there was a moment."

Why in the world did I bring this up? I should shut up and drive.

"There you go. Now it's getting interesting." She wraps the rest of the breakfast into a napkin and looks at me.

"Nothing personal, Rita, but I'd rather not talk about it."

"That's fine, I understand. After all, we've only just met."

Finally, she gets it.

Five minutes later she says, "About that man you mentioned, what happened exactly?"

"Do you never give up?"

"It's a long drive. And I don't like small talk."

One thing we have in common.

"Are you sure you want to hear the boring story of my life?"

"I'd be honored."

So, I tell her the basics about Julian, the split, and how our surprise meeting threw me off.

"And now what? Would you take him back?"

It sounds wrong.

"He's getting married. He brought her to the party."

She lets out a small sigh.

"Well, do you have a plan in mind and, most importantly, is he worth it? Otherwise, don't waste your time, dear. Love and revenge don't mix."

I don't think revenge has anything to do with it. Of course, there were days when I cursed him. That's perfectly normal, my friends said. And yes, in a perfect world I would have found someone else before he ambushed me with his wedding, even if that's petty and immature. And no, I don't want them to live happily ever after. Who'd want that after being dumped? I'm not a saint. Could our love be as carefree as it was before the breakup? I think it can. If we both really want it.

"I wouldn't call it a plan, but I'm going to a party at his house next week. Me and the guy he assumes is my boyfriend." That sounds so cheesy.

"What makes him think that? Did you hire an escort?"

"Of course not."

Of course, I did, and I'm paying for it right now, driving through Nevada in a musty RV that's turned into a therapy couch. I feel like we're one session away from dissecting my childhood. Rita takes an orange from her bag.

"What exactly do you do at the language school?"

"I was hired as an executive assistant. Now that my boss spends more and more time overseas, I'm kind of a managing director." It sounds much bigger when I say it out loud.

"Do you love it?"

I look straight ahead, but I feel Rita's eyes on me.

"Love is a strong word."

"You have no idea how short life is. Love should be felt in everything you do. If you're not jumping out of bed in the morning, passionate about life, you'll end up like those shriveled prunes at the Golden Pond." She sounds agitated.

"What's the Golden Pond?"

We're on a curvy road and I can only look at her for a split second. She rips the peel off an orange.

"Nothing, just a place."

"Do you live there?"

She looks out the window and says, "Beautiful to see the desert from up here, isn't it?"

"You know, Rita, we're stuck in here for a good part of the day, there's no radio, and you know everything about me, so what's your story?"

She chews her mandarin for about a mile.

"Golden Pond Retirement Village, Yuba City," she says. "And it's not what it sounds like. No village, no pond. Just two hundred and fifty seniors stuffed in cubicles the size of this camping van."

"Why do you live there when you don't like it? Wait—Yuba City, so it was you after all, the missing lady for the return bus?"

She nods and moves her jaw from right to left which makes her look like a deer munching on a leaf.

"So, you escaped?" My head turns quickly between her and the road.

"We're not locked up there. I can go wherever I want. Just happened to miss the bus last night, that's all."

There's that little smile in her voice again.

"I grew a little tired of the three Bs—Bingo, Bible, Birthdays."

Newspaper articles about missing seniors come to mind. *Last seen wearing a gray sweater and brown slippers.*

"Won't they be looking for you?"

"It will be a while before they notice, and by then I'll be back anyway. Eating in the dining hall is optional. I prefer to do my own cooking."

"Did you have this little adventure planned?" I point at her oversized bag.

"No, not really. I'm always prepared."

"Prepared for what?"

"For an adventure, Paula. Something to get me out of this end-of-life trap, if only for a day. I just had my seventy-sixth birthday, and every month one of us is leaving the place through the backdoor. In the gray van that says Evergreen Funeral Services."

She looks out the side window.

"That's why I sign up each time they offer a casino trip. It's not about the gambling. It's the idea that anything can happen. Like us, meeting last night, and now we're on this road trip together. Isn't that exciting?"

"By trip you mean a one-way to Vegas, right?"

"Of course, dear. In another six hours we each go our own way, I promise."

"Don't get me wrong, Rita, you're a nice lady, and I enjoy our conversations."

"Don't feel bad, I understand."

None of us says anything for a while, but it's a rather awkward silence.

"So, what's in your adventure bag?" I ask.

"Change of clothes, tennis shoes, passport, couple of containers, the usual."

The usual? I don't have any of that in my daily purse.

"What are the containers for, a roadside Tupperware party?"

"You can never bring enough containers. Frank and I would always end up finding things on our travels."

What things, apples? Body parts? I wish she was more normal.

"Seashells, rocks, birds that fell out of their nest. One time we found a baby rabbit that we fed with a dropper until it was strong enough to survive."

Seashells are harmless. I shouldn't always expect the worst.

"Also, I don't like to buy overpriced food, so I always bring my own snacks."

Rita takes out a pocket mirror and dabs some color onto her heart-shaped lips. She must have been a beauty in her day. Her face is symmetrical with a narrow nose and perfectly shaped eyebrows. She has wrinkles, of course, but her whole being is so vivacious that she seems ageless.

"It's hard to believe that there was a time when Tahoe attracted all the big names in show business. Sinatra, Marilyn, the Kennedys, they were all there."

She pulls the zipper of her cosmetic pouch.

"Frank was a pianist, you know. One of the best. He was booked every single night of the week. Casinos, piano bars, he sang, too. At one time we lived in a suite at the Sands, can you believe that?"

She smiles while her mind seems in a different space.

"We stayed in Vegas until he got those health problems."

Rita fumbles with the button of her blouse.

"It started with a cough. The doctor said not to worry, the X-ray looked fine. Take it easy for a few days, he said. Get a humidifier for the bedroom. But the cough wouldn't go away. Eventually they stopped hiring him. Who wants a piano player who gets coughing fits in the middle of the show? I started waitressing while Frank stayed home. Then the doctor said the desert was too dry, so we moved to the Bay area. We thought that Frank would find work in San Francisco once he got better. He died three months later."

"I'm so sorry, Rita."

"The cigarette smoke in the bars. He never smoked, my Frank, but that's what did it."

"How long have you been on your own?" I wish I could hug her now, but the road's too narrow to stop.

"Seven years." She crosses both arms in front of her and then puts her hands back in her lap. "I stayed in the house we rented and worked late shifts at the IHOP. When my brother passed away, he left me some money and his place at the Golden Pond."

Rita pulls a tape out of her bag.

"This is him playing. I always carry it with me. Would you like to hear it?"

I'm glad for the distraction and start the cassette player.

Beautiful ballads fill up the motor home and take us to another era. Rita closes her eyes and hums along. I think the trip will be all right. She's a sweet old lady and my gut feeling must have been wrong.

CHAPTER Eight

The fuel gauge is in the red and I haven't seen a gas station for miles.

"I need to use the washroom. Would you mind stopping there?" Rita says as we pass the sign for a rest area with services.

The coffee booth is closed until April and the vending machine is out of order. We're the only vehicle in the parking lot. Rita heads for the ladies' entrance at the other end of the building and I try to call Dan again. The receptionist puts me through to his room, but he's not there. I hang up without leaving a message.

This is the warmest day of the trip so far. I open all the windows and take a yogurt from the fridge, then step outside and walk around the parking lot. It's a treat to see the sun in November.

A good twenty minutes has passed since we got here and Rita's still not back. Maybe I should go and check if everything's okay. I lock the RV door and start walking to the washroom.

"Rita?" I call as I get closer.

No reply. All I hear is the grinding of my shoes on the gravel. I'm almost by the door now.

"Hello, Rita, are you in here?"

I wait before I walk in. There are only five stalls. As I walk by them, I push the doors open one by one. Nothing. It's cold in here, and musty. Where is she? I go back outside and call her name. Five more minutes, then I'll call the police.

As I take out my phone, I see somebody walking toward me from the treed area beside the building. Strange, there was no other car in the parking lot when we pulled in, and this is not a hiking area. The person is getting closer and waves at me. I squint against the sunlight, rub my eyes, and look again. No doubt, this is Rita. She has a rope in her hand and drags something black and furry along.

"Where did you go? I was looking for you," I shout in her direction.

She's almost caught up with me, a mangy creature by her side.

"Look, Paula, the poor thing was tied to a tree. I heard him crying all the way till here, so I went to take a look. He must have been out there for a while."

The thing lies down and I can't even see its face.

"What is this? A dog?"

"Of course, it's a dog." She pulls a burr from his beard and loosens the rope around his neck.

"And what are you doing here with a dog? Don't you want to go to Vegas?"

I turn around and walk back to the RV.

"This little sweetheart was left out to die. Look at this, the neck is all sore, he must be hurting. We have to take care of him."

"No, we don't."

"Where's your heart, Paula?"

"My heart's right here, but I'm not responsible for this dog. People abandon pets all the time. I can't help that."

The dog can barely keep up with us.

"But now we found this one, we're his only chance to survive. That makes us responsible."

She's wrong. I can't save the world and all its homeless dogs and cats and people. I can't help it that old age homes are awful, and that people die. Last night I was tired, and Rita overwhelmed me. But this time I know what's right. I'm not responsible for her. We're at the motorhome now and Rita holds on to the rope.

"He's not coming with us." I unlock the door and step inside.

"Would you please pass me my bag then? I'm staying."

"You can't stay out here. Who's going to pick you up in the middle of nowhere?"

"Thanks for everything and have a good trip, Paula."

Her eyes meet mine for a split second, then she looks the other way.

"Rita, come on. Why don't you tie him to the bench over there and I'll call animal control?"

She stays put without blinking, like Lincoln at Mount Rushmore.

I reach across the passenger seat and lift her bag. It's heavier than I expected.

"I'm sorry, but I can't do this. Take care, Rita."

Her belongings in one hand, the dog's rope in the other, she walks back toward the washroom. I watch her in the mirror and hope that she'll come to her senses, but she doesn't turn once. When I drive away from the rest area, I feel relieved that I can focus on my own business again. Go to Vegas, get rid of the bass, drive home.

I haven't made more than three miles when I feel a punch in my stomach. What if something happens to her? How could I have left an old lady at that forlorn rest stop all by herself? I hit the brakes so hard that the bathroom door opens and bangs against the kitchen counter. The road's not made for U-turns and by the time I'm done chopping back and forth to get around, the curtains have rocked themselves closed and the China's in pieces.

Rita and the dog are seated on a bench like an old couple. Neither of them move as I get out of the motorhome.

"How do we know he doesn't have some horrible disease?" I point at the dog and he flinches back in fear.

"We don't," she says.

"We'll take him to the nearest pound."

His overgrown face turns to Rita, then he cautiously takes a step forward to sniff my hand. I don't want to pet him, he looks so dirty. He sniffs around the bench for a while and sits down to pee.

"Now, I'm not an expert, but aren't males supposed to lift a leg?" I look at Rita.

"Maybe he's too weak." She shrugs and feeds him a Diamond Mountain dinner roll from her bag.

The dog that's about to board my father's motorhome is either too old or too sick, since he moves in slow motion and can hardly make it up the steps. I push from behind while Rita lures him inside with more food. A stinging mix of foul breath and urine is filling the RV. No wonder we never had pets.

"Thank you," Rita says as I turn back onto the road.

I keep my eyes ahead. "You're welcome."

And that is definitely the last time I'm doing her a favor.

The next sign announces a gas station in three miles.

"You did the right thing, Paula. If everyone showed compassion for just one other being, the world would be a different place."

"Nice try to distract from the smell."

She rubs his ears and the dog moves in closer. His tail is slowly coming up from underneath his belly.

"He likes us," Rita says.

"Don't get too attached, it'll be bye-bye before dinner."

The gas station offers full-service only. A friendly young guy with a baseball hat starts to clean the windshield while the tank's filling up.

"Excuse me, is there a dog pound in this town?"

"No miss. It's not even a town."

"Do you maybe know of anyone who's missing a dog?" I point up to the driver's seat, where a panting furball stands with two paws on the dashboard.

He shakes his head and keeps wiping.

"So, I assume, there wouldn't be a veterinarian either in your, um, village?"

"Nah. Next town over, there's more people. The doctor's in the strip mall at the first intersection. Nice fellow, my girlfriend takes her gerbil there."

I pay him with the cash from the coffee jar and we're on our way.

Two-thirty. We don't talk much until we get to the turn-off for Cannington. The animal hospital is tucked in between a Dollar Barn and the Dragon King Restaurant. A matronly woman in her fifties is about to turn the sign from OPEN to CLOSED. I wave frantically as I run across the parking lot. Rita and the dog follow at their own pace. The woman pulls out a watch from the pocket of her zebra-print scrubs and opens the door just wide enough for her head to fit through.

"Wednesdays we close at three." She ends with a crescendo on the three and points at the opening hours.

"I'm sorry, but it's sort of an emergency," I say. "We found this dog tied to a tree not far from here and we don't know what to do. Could someone please look at him?"

"I can't make that decision," she says and starts rubbing a brown stain on her shirt.

"Would there be someone around who can?"

Still rubbing, she mumbles something and lets go of the door. I take this as an invitation and follow her inside. It smells like a goat pen. She disappears behind a curtain and Rita takes a seat. After a couple of minutes, the woman comes back from behind the curtain, strolls to her desk, and starts the computer. She's not a people person.

"What kind of animal?" she asks me.

"Dog. Obviously."

"Breed?"

"Mix."

"Mix of what?" She taps her nails on the keyboard and looks up at the ceiling.

"As I told you, we just found him. We don't know anything."

She lifts her body slightly to assess the mutt's pedigree. "Terrier mix," she says to herself and resumes typing. Then she bends forward again, this time a little longer, and hits the delete key a couple of times. "Shepherd-poodle-terrier mix, black."

For someone who can't wait to go home, she's extremely attentive to detail.

"Date of birth?"

"We don't have that information either. Is this really necessary?" I can barely contain my anger.

"What's the name of the animal?"

I'm about to explode.

"Walter," Rita says.

The assistant takes a clipboard and disappears behind the curtain.

"Walter?" I hiss at Rita. "Who's Walter?"

"It just popped up. I don't know why. It's someone at Golden Pond."

What a horrible name. And I don't even care for the dog.

"He always cheats at Bingo."

I look around the waiting room. Canned food, tick tweezers, a poster depicting the life cycle of heartworms, and some hand-written ads for pet sitting. The donation jar for the local Spay & Neuter program is empty. Even though I know that it's just Rita and me in this room, I feel as if someone's watching. I turn to the right. A green and yellow bird, too large to be cute, sits motionless in an unlocked cage and stares at us.

"Give kissie," it screeches when its button eyes meet mine. "Give Coco kissie."

There's something threatening in the tone. I look away and hope the crazy talk will stop.

"Give kissie. Give Coco kissie."

A second bird comes shooting down from nowhere, brushes my forehead with the tip of its wings, and flies into the cage with a loud scream.

"This is a madhouse," I whisper to Rita.

"Right?" she says. "With the door left open, why would they volunteer to fly *into* the cage?"

That's what she finds strange around here?

Finally, the striped assistant comes back, and we're being ushered into the consultation room to meet Dr. Ramirez, a refined looking man with a soft accent. He wears a light blue tie underneath his lab coat and looks somewhat out of place.

"So, what's your story?"

He bends down and holds out a treat. I look at Rita, but she's focused on an anatomy chart above the exam table.

"Where did you say you found him?"

"At a rest area, about forty minutes north of here. He was tied to a tree and my friend heard the whining. I just want to make sure we're not dealing with rabies, or fleas, or whatever they can have."

Dr. Ramirez takes a thorough look inside the snout, feels alongside the belly, then gets his stethoscope.

"The only thing we noticed is, he moves slowly."

I look at Rita, who is unusually quiet, still staring at the poster as if she'll be quizzed on zoology terms.

"The dog is perfectly fine. It's a female by the way." Dr. Ramirez feeds another treat to the dog. "She's about eight years old. And congratulations, she's about to have puppies."

Rita shoots around and her surprise is real this time, I think.

"She's two, three days from giving birth, but I could be slightly off. You'd better get prepared."

He grabs something from the bookshelf.

"Here's a little brochure. It tells you everything you need to know. At the back, there's a list of things you should get, like blankets, towels, plastic bags. The dog lets you know when it's time. And as far as I can tell there are three puppies."

He takes off his lab coat and hangs it in a closet.

"But, Doctor, you don't understand. This is not our dog." I sound like a GPS after a missed turn.

"Are you planning to take her back to the tree then?"

"We were hoping to find a pound for him. Her, I mean. I've been driving for almost three days and need to be in Vegas tomorrow. I cannot possibly have a dog. I'm from Canada."

"What about you, ma'am?" Dr. Ramirez calmly asks and turns to Rita. "Are you from Canada as well?"

"I live in Yuba County, sir. They don't allow dogs where I live."

"Well, ladies." He looks at the cat-shaped clock above his desk. "I understand that this is quite a surprise for you, and to answer your previous question, we don't have a municipal pound. There is a lady who takes in abandoned animals and tries to re-home them. I can give her a call for you, but don't keep your hopes up too high. We have way too many strays."

He opens the door and talks to his assistant.

"Rosie, can you find Ms. Donaldson's number and put me through, please? You can go home after that. I'll lock up after these ladies."

"Thanks, Doc, see you in the morning."

Dr. Ramirez cuts off the rope from around our dog's neck and puts ointment on her sore skin.

"Apply this twice a day until the redness is gone."

He opens a drawer and pulls out a handful of entangled collars and leashes. "Let's see if we have something in here that fits her."

The phone rings and he starts explaining our situation to the dog lady. He keeps nodding. While I cannot understand what she says, I have the feeling it's a no.

"Okay then, thanks anyway, and good luck with your pack." He sets the phone down. "Like I said, her home is maxed out and she can't help you today, unfortunately." He scribbles something on the back of the puppy brochure. "This is my cell number. Call me if you have any more questions. Otherwise, be assured that it will be an experience you'll never forget."

He puts a green collar around Walter's neck and hands me a leash.

"Give her one of these right away. She could use an early dinner." He takes three cans of dog food from the shelf. "If you'll excuse me now, I have to check on a horse."

"How much do we owe you, Doctor?" Rita unfolds her wallet.

"This one's on the house, ma'am. Have a good night."

Rita puts a bill into the donation bin.

"Oh, and there's a groomer at the Fairview Mall in Bracebridge. This mat must come off before she gives birth."

We walk to a sliver of grass beside the Dragon King. Rita beside me, clutching her bag. I feel like a mother who has just learned that her teenage daughter has gotten knocked up.

"Did you honestly think she was a boy when you found her?"

"Maybe it was the beard."

Walter-the-girl sniffs around a dying evergreen and sits down for the world's longest pee.

The smell of homeless dog and musty carpet is a fresh breeze compared to the vet's office. Rita goes straight to her seat. She has a way of doing things so quietly, even the buckle of the old seatbelt slides into its counterpart like a silver bell. When she walks, it's as if her feet don't even touch the ground. I got startled a few times when I didn't hear her move and then she was right behind me. There's something fragile about her now, like a child that's been scolded and sent to her room. She completely disappears behind the broad backrest of the captain's chair.

"Don't feel bad, Rita." I put my hand on her shoulder. "I'm not fond of the detour, but I'll survive, really."

She holds on to my hand, smiles and nods to herself.

I open a can of dog food and empty it into a bowl. It's gone in three seconds. Looking at the map it's obvious that Bracebridge isn't on our way at all. I look down at Walter who's now curled up by my feet. A visit to the gynecologist takes a lot out of you.

"There it is, Fairview Mall, turn right at the next intersection."

Rita has been reading the map without glasses and saw the mall before me. She must be some sort of super senior.

As I lock the door of the RV, I accidentally step on the dog's paw. She yelps in pain.

"Oh no, little dog. I'm sorry, I didn't see you there."

I bend down and crouch in front of her. She puts her paw on my knee and looks at me. Her face is cute, with those big eyes and the stubborn beard. I pat the tip of her ear and she seems to like it. She buries her snout in my sleeve and I stroke her neck, her head, and the length of her back. Her fur is knotted and greasy, like an old blanket that's been left outside all winter. On our way to the entrance, she walks between us, almost keeping up with our pace.

"Please be careful, she's expecting," I say to the groomer, who is so skinny that his apron's wrapped around twice. He can't be more than twenty. A spider tattoo on one hand and a peace sign on the other.

"Pregnant bitch, got it." He nods and points at the list of services. "Regular, premium or deluxe bath?"

"We're not familiar with your options," Rita says.

"Regular bath and cut starts at twenty-nine. Premium includes oatmeal shampoo for sensitive skin and a nail trim. Deluxe comes with a free toothbrush, lavender finish, and fifteen percent off selected winter coats and bandanas."

"We'll go with the premium, please."

I pay thirty-eight dollars and hand him the leash.

"Anal gland cleaning's complimentary for new customers."

"No," we both shout at the same time.

"I should stay with her," Rita says. "We don't want her to go into labor from all the stress."

Despite the big sign that says Canine Customers Only, Rita tries to squeeze herself through the narrow opening that separates the drop-off area from the grooming tables. The groomer must sense that there's no arguing with Rita, so he opens the gate and lets her in.

"I'll get some of the things Dr. Ramirez mentioned, just in case," I say to her. "And Rita? No more surprises, please, I'm maxed out."

When I get back to the grooming station, a very different dog awaits me. The collar hangs loosely around her bony neck. She's standing on stork-like legs, her ears wiping the floor as she sniffs up every inch of her new world. Her baby belly shows without the matted coat.

The dog stylist says that her fur was a solid lump, which explains the buzz cut. "It's not too cold out, she'll be fine." He feeds her a treat and opens the gate.

"Is there a dog pound nearby?" I ask him.

He tilts his head and looks like a lost puppy himself. "The Bracebridge Humane Society at the other end of town, in the industrial park. But they're closed now. After hours you gotta call the cops."

Rita keeps shaking her head as I unpack my purchases. Towels and blankets, a ten-pound bag of kibble food—grain-free with freeze dried bits of raw duck and extra protein—a set of bowls in a stand, and a rubber toy. I spread out the map and try to find the best way to get us back on the highway.

"You bought all of this for a dog that you're sending off to the pound?" she asks and squeaks the blue penguin.

"She still needs to eat."

I grab a Coke from the fridge and crack it open. The soda shoots out and floods the map south of Oregon. Good thing I'm not superstitious.

"There's a commercial campground about three hours from here." I dab Nevada with a dog towel. "We can get a good night's sleep and still be in Vegas tomorrow morning. Then we'll take her to the animal shelter, I'll meet with the guy, get rid of the bass, and finally drive back home. I can drop you wherever you like. What do you think?"

No reply. Rita's sound asleep on the couch with the hairless dog curled up against her belly. I wrap the seatbelt around the two of them and cover them with a blanket. Then I stow everything and start the motor.

With just a slice of a moon and vintage headlights, I can't go as fast as I'd like. It's nine on the dot when I pull into the Desert Springs RV Park in Lanigan, Nevada. I choose a corner spot near the clubhouse and turn off the engine. With Rita far off in dreamland, I close the curtains all around, turn on the furnace, and grab the flashlight.

The door opens with a squeak and I step out into the cool air. It feels like the longest day of my life. I stretch my arms from side to side and inhale deeply. The quiet of the night is a prized luxury after three days of engine noise. My feet sink into the sand as I attach the water hose and start filling the tank. When I step back inside, Rita wakes up.

"I don't even remember lying down. Where are we?"

"At a campsite not far from Vegas. I can't see much, but it sure feels like desert."

Walter stretches all four paws and lets out a long sigh.

"Would you care for a ramen soup?" I hold up the package and start the kettle.

"I may have just the right drink to go with it."

She digs in her bottomless bag and fills two camping mugs with wine from a reusable bottle.

“Cheers to new friends and a dog.” She takes a sip and looks as if she’s bitten into a lemon. “Eww. It’s almost not worth the trouble anymore.”

“Everything today has been a first for me, including this.” I point at the words on her plastic bottle that say Yuba City Community College.

“You saw how they throw free booze around at the casino. I just can’t drink that much at once. Every second round goes in here, for dinner at the Golden Pond.”

“Don’t they have cameras at the gambling hall?”

“Not below my knees,” Rita says.

She savors the instant soup as if it were a five-course dinner.

“Look at the souls you’ve saved today,” she says. “And it’s not even midnight.”

I look at the sleeping dog. She deserves a nicer name.

“The vet said three days until her due date, didn’t he?”

“Don’t worry, it’ll be fine. Look at her, sleeping like an angel. She doesn’t look like a dog that’s about to give birth.”

I refill both our glasses, and soon our wine tasting turns into a yawn-off.

“You can get ready for bed, Rita. I’ll take her for a quick walk.”

“Let me come with you, we’ve been sitting all day.”

The tiny moon is behind a cloud when we walk to the other end of the campsite. The dog is a bit hesitant at first, but once she realizes that we’re not dumping her in the woods, she starts to relax and trots beside us.

“Scorpions don’t come out at night, right?” I ask Rita.

“You’d better leave your shoes on.”

Not the answer I’m hoping for.

"Do you smell sulfur?" she asks. "We must be close to thermal springs." She picks up her pace and I tag along.

"There, I thought so. You found us a campsite with its own hot pool." She feels along the fence until she finds a gate.

"When was the last time you went skinny dipping?" she asks and opens the latch.

"In a blow-up pool when I was three."

"It's about time then."

I can see her silhouette in the dark as she unbuttons her blouse.

"Rita, we can't do that," I whisper. "Let's come back here in the morning, before we leave."

Splosh.

"Rita?"

"Ah, that alone was worth the trip." Her voice is trailing off.

I'm standing on the other side of the fence, clenching the leash.

"Don't worry, Paula. It's not that deep. And there's no one around."

Reluctantly, I tie the dog to the fence and open the gate.

"You'll sleep like a baby."

I must be close to the water as I can feel the mist on my face. It would be nice to soak in hot water, move around a little. I slide out of my shoes and socks. The ground is damp and slippery. I quickly peel out of my clothes and fold everything into a neat pile by the fence. The cold air sends shivers all over my body. I carefully set one foot in front of the other until I find a wooden railing. A few uneven rocks lead me down and into the water.

"Isn't it spectacular?" Rita's voice sounds closer now.

The warm water carries me like a cloud. I float on my back and stare into the night sky. The new moon is just pushing free of the clouds.

Luna. That's a nice name for our dog, soft and gentle. Luna.

I drift along until the last thought has left the hamster wheel of my mind. Almost.

CHAPTER Nine

We wake up early the next morning and are on our way before eight. The campsite had decent Wi-Fi and I wrote down the address of an animal shelter in Vegas before we left. I try not to think of Luna's trusting eyes and her gentle wake-up lick this morning.

The route through the desert is stunning, and my regular life seems light years away. With a bit of imagination, the sandy hills that frame the road look like animal shapes or faces. It's so alive, despite the sparse vegetation. The thermometer says 41°F, but the amber glow between the earth and the sun creates the illusion of a hot summer day.

"How are you planning to get back home?" I ask Rita after a stretch of silence.

She shrugs and looks straight ahead.

"Do you know where you'll be staying?"

No reply. I'm not sure if she's heard me. A sudden piercing howl makes me jump in my seat.

"What was that? What's the dog doing?" I keep my eyes on the road while Rita makes her way to the back, holding onto the hanging cabinets like a flight attendant in turbulence.

"She's under the table, going in circles," Rita says.

The howling gradually turns into quiet whining. "She might be going into labor."

"Is she panting? Shivering? Building a nest?"

I had glanced briefly at the vet's brochure, and I'm not even sure of the order.

"How much time do we have left? Has the water broken yet?" I turn around and see Rita kneeling beside the table.

"Just keep driving, Paula. There's nothing else to do for now."

Nine-thirty. Why can't this mess start in three hours from now? Maybe I should find this Troy person first, go to the shelter afterward. I'm not good with blood. I should have driven to Vegas last night.

"She just vomited. Maybe she feels your stress."

I take my foot off the gas and come to a stop by the side of the road. I fly to the back of the RV and grab paper towels and water.

"What do we do now?"

I hope Rita has a plan.

"Well, where should she have the babies?" she asks and looks around. "The shower enclosure would be good. It's the right size and will keep them safe."

Right. Shower enclosure. That's good. And easy to clean. But we need more padding. When I was crossing off the shopping list, I didn't think the stack of newspapers would be that important. Turns out I was wrong. Luckily, the bottom drawer in the kitchenette holds enough recipe magazines to start a cooking channel. Sorry Mom, I'll get you new ones.

"I don't think it's time yet." Rita holds up the booklet. "Look, here it says, 'The first stage of labor can last six to eighteen hours.'"

She looks at Luna who seems calmer now. The whining has stopped. Which means my day might still be saved. Still, better to cover the floor with Martha Stewart's Baking for the Holidays.

"Do you mind if I get back behind the wheel? I cannot miss this guy again."

Rita stays under the table with Luna. We hardly make it back on the road before the retching starts again. Ten-fifteen, looks like the bass is going back to Canada. Rita gets up and puts her hand on my shoulder.

"We're not far from the city. Maybe this man can drive up to meet you here? I'll make us a coffee."

I pull over and call Max while she starts the kettle.

"Hi. No, I'm not there yet, and I won't make it by noon."

Max asks if there's a problem with the instrument.

"No, the bass is doing great."

I lift the bedspread and make sure the damn thing's still in one piece.

"It's just that I'm stuck about an hour north of the city. Long story. Could Troy possibly meet me here?"

"I'll try. But what is it? Are you in trouble?"

I tell him not to worry and he promises to call back as soon as he gets ahold of Troy. I dunk a piece of cinnamon bun into my coffee and savor the melted sugar on my tongue.

"Do you soak everything before you eat it?" Rita asks.

"Mostly croissants." I take another bite. "But I'm learning to improvise."

"Hi, it's me again." Max has his chirpy voice back. "I talked to Troy, it's no problem."

"He's driving up here to meet me?"

"Not exactly driving, but he will meet you later."

"Max, I don't have time for mystery. What are you talking about?"

He clears his throat. "Ahem, where exactly did you say you were?"

"Amargosa Desert."

"Well, that's fantastic. You know that L.A. is practically on your way, right?"

"No, it isn't."

"Which is perfect because Troy lives there. No more missing each other in hotel lobbies or deserts. He'll take the two p.m. flight from Vegas and will be waiting at his house. You call the time, he's totally cool with whatever. Didn't you always want to see Malibu, where the stars live?"

I want to kick the bass out the door.

"Paula?"

"No."

"Come on, it's just a couple of hours west. Even better, 'cause you can take the I-5 home. It's a straight line all the way up to the border. And remember, when you're back in Vancouver I'll take you to the party your ex is throwing. Jonah, Jeremy, what's his name again?"

"You're an idiot."

I throw the phone on the couch and kick my foot against the table. The dog's trembling.

"Can you believe this?" I yell out in Rita's direction.

Of course, if it wasn't for her and her save-the-world attitude, I'd be in Vegas right now. Bass delivered, no worries, home in two days.

Rita pours me another coffee, and I drink it. Maybe not the best idea, since my heart is already racing. So much waiting around for nothing. I've seen enough middle-of-nowhere for the rest of my life and I want to get somewhere. Luna's belly rises with every breath. Her eyes are closed, but she's not asleep. How I hate to sit and do nothing.

"Why do you want to go to Vegas so badly?"

For the last half hour, Rita's been fumbling with the buckle of her bag and it drives me crazy.

She sighs and looks out the window.

"And why do you always cling to this bag? Did you rob a bank or something?"

She purses her lips.

"I'm not sure this is a good time," she says.

"It's not a good time to have a pregnant dog, and it's not a good time to sit by the side of the road, and it sure isn't a good time to tell me any more bullshit."

She pulls on her blouse and straightens imaginary wrinkles.

"I want to bring Frank home."

"I don't understand."

She takes out a large Tupperware bowl and puts it on the table between us.

"Frank's ashes are in there. I want to take him back to where we had the best years of our lives."

I lean back as far as the dinette booth allows.

"You keep your husband in a salad bowl?"

She shrugs. "You wanted the truth."

She's right, this isn't a good time.

"Do you bring him everywhere?"

"Not to the grocery store, he hates shopping." She gently lifts up the lid. "Loves casinos."

To my relief, I see a blue porcelain urn tucked inside the food container. I've never seen one up close. We both stare at Frank.

"I really had no intention of inconveniencing you. When I first saw you looking all pale in your chair, I was about to get back on the bus. But then we started chatting, and you were so nice to me, and then you mentioned that you were on your way to Vegas. I'm really sorry."

"When we met in the lobby yesterday morning, had you been up all night?"

She nods. "Coffee refills and that big plate of dessert you brought me."

I feel horrible.

"We weren't poor when Frank was alive, but we hadn't saved anything for later. You know, after one of us would pass."

"But Rita, what are you going to do once we're there? And how will you get back?"

She thinks for a moment and says, "We were never big on planning, Frank and I. Things always seemed to work out."

An image of Julian pops into my mind and the same old thoughts start circling again. Was he The One? Will things work out for us as well?

The phone rings.

"What?" I yell at Max.

He takes a big breath, and I can see his big curly head in front of me, probably chewing his lip.

"My guy's famous. Top secret. I'm not even supposed to tell you."

Things are getting more interesting. I've been chasing a celebrity all along.

"Who is it, Max? Justin Timberlake?"

Malibu could be on my way.

"It's Lamar Tennan."

"Who?"

"Lamar N. Tennan? Played with The Mongrels? Before he went solo?"

Max sounds like a valley girl.

"He's like, the god of fusion jazz."

Malibu's not on my way. Totally not.

"He's been on tour since the spring, and you were following his concert venues, dummy. Didn't you see the ads everywhere?"

I hear another round of retching behind me and cut Max off.

"Do you have children?" I ask Rita while we're cleaning the floor. Luna's stomach must be empty by now.

She shakes her head. "We gave up after the third miscarriage. What about you, do you want to have family?"

"With the right man. Maybe. But how will I know?"

"You'll feel it."

"I don't have much trust in my feelings lately."

"You know it when the question wouldn't even cross your mind." Rita puts the rag away and looks out the window.

"When worrying about the future seems foolish, and when everything about him feels familiar, as if your hearts recognized one another."

I pour a heap of baking soda on the vomit stain and swallow against the lump in my throat.

"And when he tells you he was looking for you all of his life."

My cousin back home once told me when she knew. "He got me a ring after the pregnancy test showed two lines."

CHAPTER Ten

Rita lies on the bed and reads, *Messages from the Animal Kingdom*.

"Listen to this," she says. "'A dog shows up in your life to help you understand the meaning of unconditional love. Have trust that you will be protected and safe. Now is the time to be of service to others.'"

"Did you just make that up?"

"Page twenty-three," she says.

"And you really believe this?"

"I think it's a lovely concept."

I wish I'd picked up a different book. This one's ridiculous.

"Name another animal, quick, don't overthink."

"Parrot."

Rita looks puzzled until I point at her blouse.

"Oh this." She laughs. "My remedy against November blues. Let's see what it says. 'A parrot lets you know that your life is ready to take a new turn. This may be the moment to manifest your dreams.' What do you think?"

"No, and no."

I revisit the night at the casino, and now being stuck with a dog in labor. That's the dream? No way.

"All I know is that I am exactly where I want to be." Rita closes the book.

"Anybody could have used that rest area yesterday."

"But it was us."

Incoming call. Finally, it's Dan. We chat a little, he tells me that the renovations are right on schedule, and that he's bribed his son to lend him his cell phone for the day. I hear drilling in the background.

"Listen, Paula, I don't know how to break it to you." He doesn't sound at ease. "The battery is low, so I'll have to make it short. I've decided to sell the school and move to Taipei for good. I got an incredible offer to sell TalkTalk and I wish I could have told you in person."

Bam, a punch in the stomach. Out of the blue. I knew he was glad to get away after his marriage ended, but I never expected him to walk away from the school that he built up from a basement room fifteen years ago.

"Are you still there?"

"Yeah. Just digesting the news. Do I still have a job?" I force a little laugh.

"That's why I want to see you this week. I'm trying to get the new owner to keep all of you. It'll be to his advantage anyway."

Now it's me who feels nauseated.

"I'm in Nevada."

"Nevada, hmm. When are you coming back?"

"As soon as possible, believe me."

"They're holding a job fair next week and everyone has to go through a new hiring process. I told him what an asset you've been to the company. I'm sure that once he meets you in person, he'll give you the job right away."

I'm mad, and disappointed, even though I know that Dan's trying to take care of us. He's the nicest person I've ever worked for, and I want to keep him as my boss. Plus, new hiring process means new-hire starting salary. Just what I need.

"What about Valentina?"

"Well, it's hard to find a native Portuguese speaker, so I think her job is safe."

Of course, it is. Only a blind and deaf moron would let Valentina go. But people like me, with a degree in French like a gazillion others, and zero hotness? Back to the temp agency at minimum wage, answering the phone for assholes in suits. Which means I'll have to move to a cheaper place or find a roommate. Or both.

"Don't panic, Paula. I'm meeting with the buyer in one hour. I'm sure we can work something out. You'll hear from me as soon as I know more."

Rita kneels next to Luna who's panting heavily. I join her on the ground and share the news.

"Does the job mean a lot to you?"

"Yes, of course it does. I like going to work every day, I like my colleagues, the students, we always have fun. Also, I'm still paying off my student loan, and rentals in Vancouver are crazy expensive."

"One thing at a time." Rita takes my hand. "First you need to find this musician. That's money in your hands. Maybe we can still make it to Vegas before he leaves."

There's a knock on the passenger side window. I jump up and peek through the blinds.

Highway Patrol.

A rush of blood shoots through my system, I don't even know why.

"Keep both hands visible," Rita says before I open the slider. "And don't move fast."

"Good afternoon, can I see your license, please?"

A middle-aged trooper stands about three feet away. My nerves come down a little when he takes off his sunglasses. With his round face and reddish curls, he looks more like an Irish pub owner. He watches carefully as I open my wallet and hand him the plastic card.

"Any reason you're parked on the side of the highway?"

"We had to take care of a sick dog," I answer.

"Do you have the registration for this vehicle?"

I stand up and look for the piece of paper in the bin above my seat. Meanwhile, he asks Rita for her ID and our destination. He scribbles something on a yellow pad, rips it off and hands it to me.

"This is a warning for parking on the shoulder. No need to do anything, it's not a fine. But you cannot stay parked here."

I glance at the page and fold it into the registration papers.

"Now, what kind of dog trouble do you have?"

"She's about to give birth," Rita says. "The driving upsets her stomach, we believe."

"May I come in?" he asks, signals something to his colleague in the car, and walks around to the door.

I look at Rita before I unlock. She shrugs and doesn't seem to find anything unusual.

"That's one skinny dog," he says and bends down to pet her. "My wife's a dog nut, three dachshunds, sometimes a foster dog or two, I've seen it all."

Our lucky day, given the circumstances.

"I tell you what. There's a rest area about eight miles from here. You can stay there as long as you need. Just no overnight camping."

"Thank you, we'll do that," I say with relief.

"Have a good day, ladies."

He puts his sunglasses back on and steps outside.

"You may want to think about having her neutered," he says. "Too many strays around here."

On the way to the rest area Luna throws up twice, and I give up on the idea of catching the famous Lamar before his flight leaves. We set up two lawn chairs and enjoy a late lunch of leftovers. Maybe it's the warmth of the sun, or maybe it's a belly full of food, but the panic I felt half an hour ago has faded and turned into exhaustion. I rest my head against the chair, but the cell phone stops me from dozing off.

"Please surprise me with good news, Dan."

"At least I bought you some time, four days to be exact. The appointment with the lawyer is Wednesday morning, and Luke, the buyer, agreed to meet you right after that. He said if it was love at first sight, he would buy you along with the business. His words, not mine. Don't worry, Paula, he's a good guy, just a weird sense of humor. He's Australian."

I'm tired of Aussies taking things away from me.

"Just make sure to be here on time. If all goes well, he'll keep you on as the managing director, as he's planning to go back and forth for a while."

"I'll be back as soon as I can. When are you leaving?"

"My flight is booked for Thursday."

"I'll miss you, Dan."

The phone is still in my hand when Max calls again.

"So, what do you think?" he asks.

"Well, let's see. The language school's being sold. I have no job unless I pass an interview for the position I've already had for seven years, and a stray dog is giving birth in my father's camper."

"Is that a metaphor?"

"It's a shepherd-poodle-terrier-mix, black!"

"So, that's a no?"

"There's a lot going on right now, Max, and your bass is not on the top of my list."

"It's just that Lamar wants to know when."

"Oh, Lamar wants to know? Tell him to go back in time and meet me at the front desk the day before yesterday."

CHAPTER Eleven

"**So, about this** man you mentioned earlier. Did he leave you?" Rita asks as we soak up the late afternoon sun. "Do you want to fix my life now?"

I'd rather talk about the weather.

"Does it need to be fixed?" she asks.

"I'm not sure anymore."

"If it was all up to you, Paula from Vancouver, would you want him back in your life?"

"Maybe. I don't think so."

I hear the words and they don't feel right. Not if I'm being honest with myself.

"Yes, Rita, I want him back. I haven't stopped thinking of him since that party. Sure, he said some stupid things, but so did I. And I know him, I really do."

My mind goes back to the night at Valentina's. The way he looked at me. How long he held me in his arms until his girlfriend came back.

"We're not over yet."

"At least you know what you want," she says.

We have a history, we still having feelings for each other despite what happened. He writes Christmas cards to my mother. So what if Rita has her theory about first meetings. Just because it worked for them, doesn't mean every love story in the world has to start like that.

"Of course, it hurt when he broke up with me. Although technically, he didn't even break up with me. It was me who gave up on us when he told me he'd kissed another woman."

He spent the night with her, but Rita doesn't have to know every detail.

"Have you never given someone a second chance?" I ask.

"Many times." Rita squints at the sun. "Just not when it comes to love."

"You would never have forgiven Frank, whatever the circumstances?"

"Oh sure, I would have forgiven." She smiles her sweetest old lady smile. "And then I would have left him."

"Why forgive when you're leaving? There's no point."

"Forgiveness is for your own good, Paula. So that the past doesn't weigh you down. But I would never stay with someone who hurt my heart."

She leans back and seems to be in a different space.

"Our life together went by like this." She snaps her fingers. "One day we met, and then he was gone. It's the years without him that feel like eternity."

"How did you make it through after Frank passed?"

"There are weeks that I don't remember at all." She twists the sleeve of her blouse into a knot, then releases it.

"I may have gotten up, or not. I may have cooked, but then not even touched the food. Day or night, it was all the same since the love of my life had been reduced to a blue urn. Eventually, there came a day when I was able to think clearly."

"And you found joy again?"

"I decided to end my life."

I sit up straight.

"I chose a Sunday afternoon. Cleaned up the house, put on a nice dress, the pills all lined up in front of me. Frank's doctor had been generous with morphine." She clears her throat before she goes on. "I sat in my usual spot at the table, facing the street. And then something strange happened. A woman walked by with her two children, one in a stroller and one bouncing alongside his mother, maybe three, or four." She stops and smiles. "I can still see their faces. The mother must have said something to the little boy who burst out laughing. He took her hand and jumped along with this carefree, contagious joy that only children know. And in that split second, I had the desire to laugh again. Isn't that crazy? I put the pills back in the bathroom and opened the windows. Not today, I said to myself. I need to laugh one more time."

I get up and wrap my arms around her.

"Frank would never come back, and the sadness was still there. But it had a little crack."

I hold her tightly, my cheek against hers.

"You have a good heart, Paula."

Her skin feels cold. I grab two blankets and wrap one around Rita. A flood of emotion washes over me. I feel so lonely, and sad. I want to cry, but I can't. I feel sad for Rita and her pain, and for this dog under the table, for the old people at the casino, whose eyes looked so hopeless, and for my mother who lives love through the pages of a book, and my father who'll never make it to Costa Rica.

"Frank and I had a friend. His name was Joe, Joe di Lucca. His wife died six months after they got married. It was sad, really. He was lost. Started drinking and then had a complete breakdown. His sister convinced him come to India with her. In the early sixties, imagine that. People thought Joe was nuts, selling everything he owned to go on a trip. Anyway, they traveled to Rishikesh, lived in an ashram, the whole bit. Joe stayed there for two years. I still have the letters he wrote us. He studied meditation and became an instructor himself. Eventually, he moved back here and opened a center for spiritual healing somewhere on the Oregon Coast." She waves her hand vaguely in the direction we've come from. "One day, out of the blue, I thought of him and how he had turned his life around. That same day there was a flyer in the mail about a new meditation program at our community college. I went to the free class and stayed for years."

"You meditate every day?" I ask her.

"Not as much as I used to. It's more like Tylenol, whenever my head gets too heavy."

Like mine right now.

I must have fallen asleep. At first Rita's whispering fits my dream perfectly. Then it stops making sense.

"The first puppy's here."

I jump up from the lawn chair and follow her inside. Rita points under the table. Luna is lying on a pile of sheets, rhythmically licking a spot between her front legs. I get down on my knees and there it is, the tiniest thing, barely a handful of life, sand colored with black spots. Both eyes are closed, and the little pink feet are aimlessly kicking the air. Luna is on autopilot, oblivious of her surroundings. As if it were important for future reference, I take note of the exact time. It's 5:22 p.m.

The firstborn is determined to find food and it paddles forward with all its strength, almost swallowed by the folds of the blanket. The built-in navigation system brings it to mama's belly where it practically collapses from the struggle of the journey.

Within one hour, baby number two and three make it into the world. I don't know how long we've been sitting here. Dr. Ramirez was right. It's an experience like nothing else. I feel as if the animal's love is spreading out to us humans, making us part of something bigger. I crouch in front of the shower pan and feel bliss.

It's been dark for a couple of hours now. Every once in a while a coyote howls in the distance. I want to stay in this moment forever, but my empty stomach and the necessity to find a place for the night make me slide back into reality.

No other cars or lights around us, just an endless array of stars. We struggle to see road signs and crawl along at thirty-five miles an hour, until we see a flickering neon cactus inviting us to turn right. Twenty minutes later we're set up for the night and our celebration dinner, spaghetti with pesto, is steaming on the table. We both avoid the word animal shelter and end the day with a short walk around the campsite. Then I fall into a dreamless sleep.

CHAPTER Twelve

We arrive at the Humane Society of the Desert just before ten. The shelter is about to open, and people with leashed dogs by their side are lined up halfway around the building. We leave ours in the motorhome for now. The groomed palm trees look so pretty, and the sun burns down on the parking lot. I wish I'd brought sunglasses. No, I wish it was raining. People who dump puppies don't deserve blue skies.

After a few minutes, a woman with a clipboard puts her head through the door and asks if anybody's here for a missing pet. An older gentleman puts up his hand. His cat didn't come home last night.

"Anyone here to adopt?" the woman asks.

A gravelly bark from the front of the line is the lone answer.

"There's a box with pet surrender forms by the door. Fill it out as best as you can and have it ready when you come inside."

People speak in hushed voices. Everybody looks down, like in a funeral procession. The elderly woman in front of us has a small dog in her arms. She doesn't stop kissing the dog's head, rocking it like a baby.

"It's for the better," I say to Rita and lower my voice even more. "Can't save them all."

The solemn mood is suddenly shaken up by a blue van with an exhaust problem. It tears around the corner and pulls into one of the spots in the shade, the muffler dangling from a wire. The doors are painted with psychedelic flowers and the bumper stickers aren't subtle. *Pro Life? Go Vegan*, *Grow Your Own Fur*, and the one next to a stenciled piglet says, *Bacon Had A Mom*. The back of the van gets slammed with a bang, and the waiting line starts to move.

Rita's chatting with the lady in front of us, and they're both hunched over the tiny dog in her arms. From the corner of my eye, I see the driver of the van walking toward us. He carries a pile of empty crates and lines up behind me, phone tucked between his ear and shoulder. No smell of pot yet.

In fact, he smells rather nice. Like fresh cut wood, or grass after the rain. He's talking quietly to whoever is on the other line. A nice voice. Dark and calm. A little raspy, maybe he didn't get much sleep last night.

Rita's staring at me, her lips moving, and she's waiting for somc-thing. I don't even hear what she says.

"What?"

"Do you have a pen?" she asks and looks a little scared. "Please?"

I find one in my backpack and give it to her. "Sorry," I whisper. Shouldn't snap at Rita.

What is he doing with all those crates? Does he sell pets to labs? I still haven't seen his face. Just his sneakers. Converse, I think. Lighter than his jeans and—dammit, he saw that I was checking him out. But he smiles. At me. A pretty great smile, too.

I turn away and feel my face blush. The heat is pumping through my head and hammers against both temples. My color must be vintage merlot. Why do I still turn red as an adult? Cold. Snow. Calm. The more I want it to go away, the hotter I feel.

"Excuse me, would you mind keeping an eye on these?"

No, no, no. Please don't talk to me now, just another minute and I'll be fine. It'll pass, I know it will. I dig one fingernail into the nail bed of my thumb. It hurts like hell, but the blood in my head goes back to where it came from.

I nod while I try to think of something smart to say.

"Great." He stacks the crates beside me.

Now that he's facing the other way, I watch him walk to his van. White T-shirt and faded Levi's. Surfer hair, kind of curly. Or maybe just messy. Am I dehydrated? Is this really happening?

They say you see your whole life as a slide show at the moment of death. I'm standing here with a bleeding thumb and see my entire future. Driving around in a hippie van, a flowery meadow, us kissing, barking dogs, and low-flying airplanes.

Rita gives me a nudge and I don't know why she's in the meadow, too. Then I realize that the landing planes are real, so are the dogs. Given that we're at the entrance to a municipal shelter and the airport's five blocks away.

He returns with more crates. I hold myself a little straighter and rake through my unwashed hair.

"Dropping or adopting?" he asks.

His voice is smoother than velvet. Mine is lost.

"We found a pregnant dog," Rita says. "My friend here is from Canada and she can't bring her back."

Love you, Rita. I'm almost ready for my first word after some nodding and a lot of smiling.

"That's too bad," he says. "I guess you can come back and get her once the babies are born."

How sweet, he thinks I'm a good person.

"Yesterday."

That was my grand opener? *Yesterday*? Accompanied by the scratchy sound of clearing my throat.

"Pardon me?"

"They were born yesterday."

There, a complete sentence. Phlegm-free.

"How many do you have?" he asks.

"What?"

"Pups, how many are there?"

Why does he ask all these questions? It's hot out here. I need to sit.

"Three and their mom," Rita says.

"We run a dog rescue outside of town, that's why I'm asking."

He still looks at both of us while he talks. "We try to help these guys out whenever we can. That's what these are for." He points at the crates. "We take the very young, the very old, and the ones that need extra care. Then we find permanent homes for them. Some have stayed forever."

"That sounds like heaven," I say and keep my eyes on his so he doesn't turn to smoke and crawl back into a bottle.

Even though he speaks with a low voice, the old lady in front of us turns around and asks if he would take her dog. "Please, it would mean the world to me."

He pets the terrified bundle in her arm.

"I'm moving in with my daughter. She told me to get rid of the dog or they will."

"I am so sorry to hear that," he says. "Let me check in with the shelter manager. I honestly don't know how many dogs they have for us today."

She looks like she's going to cry.

"I'll see what I can do," he says, and puts his hand on her shoulder. "Promise."

Only three people ahead of us. I grab one of the surrender forms and start filling it in. My fingers are so cold that I can barely write my name. Breed, age, health concerns, I write down everything Dr. Ramirez told us about Luna. Behavior toward children remains blank, although I'm sure she'll make a fine family dog.

"You won't need this." The jeans model/dog savior takes the form out of my hand. "Puppies go straight from here into foster care. No need to burden them with paperwork. You can just tell me all about the dog."

The lady with the tiny dog reaches for one of the forms and puts it back the next second.

"I've had him for ten years. His name's Toto, and he's the sweetest. Please help me." She holds him up like a sacrificial lamb. The dog lets out a wailing cry.

"I'll take him," Rita says.

Toto's owner is just as perplexed as I am. She wipes her eye with one hand.

"I promise I will take good care of him." Rita caresses the little dog's ear.

The handsome stranger looks at me.

"Are all Canadians this spontaneous?" he asks in a low voice. His head's so close that I can smell his hair. Vanilla coconut.

"We only met three days ago," I say, not moving an inch. "She's not Canadian."

"I'm Ben, by the way."

"Paula."

We let the guy with the cat carrier pass. Rita's in deep conversation with Toto's owner. They hug and cry, cuddle the dog, hug some more, completely oblivious of anything that's going on around them.

Ben looks at me. Please don't ask anything, my brain is out of order. My heart beats at the speed of light, and I'm afraid I'll blush again any second.

"I'll quickly run over to the motorhome, see how the dogs are doing," I say, and start walking backward.

"I'll wait."

He is so relaxed, so confident, so, I don't know, perfect. What if something happens, and I get atrial fibrillation and pass out in the RV and he has to leave, and we never see each other again?

"Would you like to see my puppies? Sorry, that sounds weird. I mean, it might be nice for you to meet them, since you may become their foster, hmm, person."

Ben suppresses a smile. "That's exactly how I understood it."

If a man's character can be judged by the way he looks at puppies, Ben's a ten. He kneels down in front of the little family. Without being intrusive, his eyes rest on the dogs and mine rest on him. Luna is completely calm, even licks his hand.

"What do you think?" I ask as we step back outside. The midday sun burns down, even though it's the end of November.

"I'm surprised that you're a bass player," he says.

"I mean, what do you think about the dogs?"

"I can see piano, maybe saxophone."

"It's not mine."

"Good." He smiles. "I don't think the puppies will be a problem. Mom may take a little longer. Maybe you'll change your mind and come back for her."

I lock the door and we walk back toward Rita and her new friends.

"This is not the happiest place in town," Ben says. "But do you want to come in with me?"

"I do."

He picks up the crates and still manages to hold the door open for me. We stop at the glass window and he asks the girl on duty which dogs they want him to take. She shoots him her biggest smile and without taking her eyes off of him asks the lady at a desk behind her, "Linda, which dogs go to Noah's Bark?"

Despite my friendliest "hello" she ignores me completely. A middle-aged woman comes up and hugs him.

"Ben, you're heaven-sent. Did you see the line today? It's been like that all week. I gave you the code for the back door last time, didn't I? You don't have to wait at the public entrance."

"It was nice outside," he says.

Linda, Ben, and I walk along the narrow aisle, kennels on both sides. The desperate barks are chilling. Wet noses stick out through the wire. Some of the cries cut through the air like a butcher knife, while others sound feeble, as if the dogs have surrendered to their fate. They're prisoners on death row. All innocent.

We leave the building and stop at a fenced area, about the size of my kitchen. Meet and Greet, the sign says. Five dogs are jumping up and down, desperate to catch our attention. One husky, two medium-sized mutts with ears that look like antennas, a pit bull and a little fur ball that keeps getting kicked out of the way by its bigger cell mates.

"They all had their check-ups and first round of shots," Linda says. "The staffy is young, eight or nine months. We found him with burn marks and barbed wire around his muzzle."

Ben holds out his hand for the dogs to sniff.

"The Chihuahua mix is deaf. He was brought in two weeks ago, supposedly found somewhere." She uses air quotes. "He sticks close to the others. And these two, well, just look at them. They haven't stopped shaking since they arrived."

"We'll take good care of them, Linda," Ben says.

"Let me show you the puppies. We've had to keep them in the supply room for the night."

Linda leads the way past an endless row of fenced enclosures, each of them holding three or four dogs that bark for their lives. Then she opens the door into a windowless room, crammed with buckets, brooms, rolls of fencing wire, and some tools. The stench of industrial cleansers makes me cough as soon as we enter. Linda turns on the light. A tired looking dog lies rolled up in the corner of a crate and blinks against the fluorescent tube. Her head stays flat on the ground while her offspring are feeding. As we come closer, the little dogs start wiggling around, jumping on their siblings, and stretching their tiny heads toward us.

"They're definitely ready for solid food. She had nine pups when we found her. Two didn't make it. It would be great if you could take them."

We go back to the office where Ben has to sign a few forms. Then he puts the dogs on leashes and brings them to the van. My only job is carrying the little deaf dog. He sniffs my hands with great interest, then rests his head on my shoulder. How can anyone abandon this?

I ask Ben if he still thinks they'll have space for my dogs.

Instead of an answer he gives me a piece of paper with an address. "This is where we're going. I'll try not to lose you."

A little later, all the animals are secured and ready to go. The interior of the van is in much better shape than its beaten body. Each side of the loading area has a system of hooks and harnesses to keep the dogs safe. The husky is panting wildly, and Ben opens all the windows. The puppy crate is on the floor, and mom watches carefully from the passenger seat.

Of course, I could part with Luna right now, but Ben has invited us for a tour of their place, and I'll need a break anyway before I head back home. Rita's buckled in and holds Toto on her lap. He whines a little, but he seems calmer than when I first saw him an hour ago.

"I told his owner to visit as much as she wants."

"She's moving to Yuba, too?"

"It's a small world."

CHAPTER Thirteen

I feel like a race car driver as I tailgate Ben through the downtown traffic. As soon as there's a ten-inch gap, someone tries to squeeze in. This is Las Vegas? Nothing looks the way I had imagined. Everything is bigger, higher, faster. There are billboards everywhere, and trucks passing on both sides. So many flickering neon signs that I almost miss a red light.

"This is madness," I say to Rita after we come to a halt halfway across the intersection. My hands are clawed around the steering wheel.

"It has certainly grown over the years," she replies with tenderness in her voice. "We came here with our Ford Falcon packed to the roof. I remember being so happy to be driving along Las Vegas Boulevard after those horrible Chicago winters."

"What were you doing in Chicago?" I ask as the light changes to green. Ben's waiting for us in a bus bay.

"There was a situation that we wanted to get away from for a while."

"What kind of a situation, like running from the mob?" I ask, half-jokingly.

"Worse than that. Frank's first wife." She doesn't look comfortable now. "Lola."

The Barry Manilow song comes to my mind and I start to hum.

"Ironically, that's what she was, a showgirl," Rita says. "One crazy bitch showgirl."

"No way."

"Well, born Doris Frimp. Wouldn't you want to change that name, too?" She forces a smile.

"It was a typical Vegas wedding, one in the morning and too much gin. They'd known each other for a month and a half and stayed married for nine. Frank wanted to end it earlier, but she claimed to be pregnant until she ran out of excuses why her wasp waist hadn't filled in. Anyway, they divorced right before Frank and I met."

"Were you in show business as well?" I ask.

"I was a ballet dancer. I had just taken this temporary job, not exactly classical dance, and we were touring Vegas. It was meant to be for a month, but then I met my husband and stayed."

"Did you always dance?"

"Until the injury forced me to quit." She points at her knee.

"What happened?"

"April 6th, 1966, one day after my birthday, I fell down some stairs, tore a ligament, and that was the end of my dancing career."

"And after that, what did you do?" I wish I didn't have to focus on traffic at the same time.

"This and that. Worked at a law office, sold beauty products for a while. At some point Frank got so busy that taking care of his bookings became a full-time job. That's when the greedy witch flew back into our lives and we chose to leave town."

The van turns onto a private gravel road. Ben jumps out to open the wooden gate and waves us toward a shaded spot.

"Welcome to Noah's Bark," he says with pride in his voice.

When I heard the words dog rescue, I pictured some run-down building by a junk yard. This, however, looks like a fancy resort. Or a Mexican hacienda, with its colorful walls, and palm trees everywhere. Hard to believe we're in the desert. I want to be a rescue dog.

Ben opens the back of the van. "I'll just need a few minutes to get these guys settled in, then I'll show you around."

"We don't put them behind bars. They get to run around during the day." He points at a fenced-in area the size of a soccer field.

"It's an interesting social experiment, but it works. Of course, when they first arrive, we give them time to calm down and adjust. We have some amazing volunteers, and a four-legged peer counselor."

We've been walking all around the property, Ben, Rita, and I. Toto stays right beside us and hasn't stopped once to sniff.

"The view is spectacular," Rita says. "Do you live here, too?"

Ben nods. "I owe it all to one lucky night at the casino if you can believe it."

"The gambling thing actually works?" I ask.

"Not for me, I haven't won a thing in my life." He waves at someone in a volunteer shirt. "But it worked out nicely for my friend Xavier. He was here on a scholarship from Mexico and dreamed of living in his own house by graduation day. The last night of each month he'd play roulette at El Cortez on Fremont, the same numbers every time. Believe it or not, the month before commencement, Xavier walked out of there with twenty-three thousand dollars."

"In one night?" I ask.

"Pretty much. And he'd only invested a little over five hundred in total."

"And how did you end up here?"

"Xavier's extremely persuasive. He found this property, way above his price range, and got obsessed with the idea of buying this land with the half-finished house. The perfect playground for a guy who majored in architecture. It was a foreclosure, supposed to be a horse farm. Anyway, before I knew it, I was working two jobs and owned one quarter of an abandoned construction site."

"That's a busy operation for two of you," Rita says.

"Actually, we're four now. Our friend Adam came into a little bit of money around the same time. He had gone to the worst dentist in Vegas. The guy messed up so badly that the judge made him pay twenty thousand in damages. Adam wouldn't open his mouth for months, but he now lives in a south-facing suite with its own porch. And here we are. Can I get you some coffee?"

Coffee's nice, but I'd rather hear about the fourth roommate.

"Have a seat, I'll be right with you," Ben says.

We're standing in a spectacular courtyard, the kind you only see in travel books, or movies. Bright pink bougainvillea weave along the walls, a lemon tree lazes in the sun, and tropical plants of all shapes and sizes grow out of their terracotta dwellings into the wild. There's even a small swimming pool in the corner.

Rita almost disappears into the cushions of the chair. She looks peaceful, sitting there with her new companion on her lap. I take a seat beside her and squint in the sun. Perfection.

Ben comes back carrying a French coffee press and three mugs.

"How do you take your coffee?"

"Black, please," Rita says.

"Sugar and a little bit of milk for me."

"Coconut cream and maple syrup's all we've got, I'm afraid. Ava runs a tight vegan ship. You saw her van." He smiles.

I hope he didn't hear the fist that just hit me in the stomach. Ava. The fourth person who lives here. Ava and Ben, the happy couple. Or maybe not so happy, he almost seems to be afraid of her. Ava with the militant van, and the militant diet, and the perfect boyfriend in their perfect house. Or could she be the girlfriend of one of the other two guys? No, he would have mentioned it when he talked about them.

Ben leans back and folds his hands behind his head.

"So, what's your story, with the bass and all? Auditioning for a show?"

I give him the short version of my journey. "I don't have much time to spend in Vegas, I'm already off schedule."

"And you really don't want to keep Luna?" he asks. "She's such a sweet dog. You could come back and get her in three months or so. Canadians love it here, your winters are way too long."

Before I can reply, a giant dog with the head of a cow appears out of nowhere. He drinks from the pool, pees against a palm tree, and circles the table before plopping down in the shade. A trail of drool marks his every step.

"I didn't know we had guests. Hi, I'm Ava."

A stunning beauty slides into the chair next to Ben. Yellow top, cut-off jeans and running shoes. She's jaw-dropping, out-of-this-world, that's-not-even-fair beautiful and her smile is as luminous as her hair.

"The dogs you picked up are mostly in good health, Ben. The staffy needs some TLC, but I don't see any big problems. Will you or Adam be here later?" She drinks from Ben's mug. "The clinic just called. They need someone to cover the late shift."

Girlfriend Ava. Offensively beautiful animal activist Ava. She's so tiny, the sip of coffee was probably her lunch. It's time to go home and stop daydreaming about Ben. They can all stay here and save the world together.

Another phone call from Max gives me an excuse to get up and leave the group of super humans.

"Hi, favorite neighbor, how are things?" he asks. "You seemed a bit stressed yesterday, which is totally understandable, and that's why—"

"I'll do it."

"What?"

"The detour to Los Angeles, I'll go."

"What made you change your mind? Forget it, I don't even want to know. You *are* my favorite neighbor."

"It'll cost you another thousand."

"Trust me, baby, if you knew Lamar, you'd do it for free."

"Where and when?" The new me sounds like a sex worker.

"Anytime you want. I'll text you the address. He'll be at his Malibu home for the rest of the year. I'm so jealous."

"I'll let you know when I leave. I just need to make sure that Rita's fine. And the dogs. You won't believe what happened."

"Wish I had time to hear it all, Paula, but I'm at sound check. Talk to you later. Oh, and do not, under any circumstances, tell anybody his address. Lamar is a very private person. He hates fans in front of his house, and apparently, he's got a reputation for his temper. Otherwise, he's a great guy."

I want my old life back.

CHAPTER Fourteen

Ava, her dog, and I sit on the floor of the RV. After I talked to Max, she offered to have a look at the little ones before they are moved into their new space. I want to hate her, I really do, but she's too nice. She keeps asking me all kinds of questions, about the trip and Rita, and what I think of Vegas. It's more than being polite, she seems to genuinely care. On top of being kind and beautiful, she's a veterinarian with an additional degree in animal behavior.

"They're all doing well," Ava says after listening to Luna's heartbeat. "She could use a few extra pounds, but she's in good hands with us. Look at Bear." She kisses the mammoth dog on his head. "He was skin and bones when I found him. Hard to believe now, isn't it?"

She talks to someone on her phone and I kneel to rub Luna's belly. I don't know if it's this place, or my walk through the shelter, but I suddenly feel a dash of guilt. Last time I volunteered was for a bake sale at the Chartwell Retirement Chateau. I was twelve and it was part of a school assignment.

"Thanks for doing that," Ava says to the person on the other line. "I'd like to move them into the green room for now."

She slips her phone back into her shorts. "They'll be fine. You did the right thing, taking the dog with you at that rest stop."

I avoid her eyes.

"I'd like to pay you for your trouble," I say as we walk back toward the house.

"We have a donation box by the entrance. Or, if you could spare an hour or two, we could use every hand today. Two of our regular volunteers are on a school trip and I have no idea where the boys are."

I guess she means the gambler and the dental mess.

"I'm sorry, but I should really get on my way now. The headlights on the Winnebago are useless in the dark."

"Did my brother mention that we also rent out guest rooms?" she asks.

I stop dead in my tracks.

"Your brother?"

Ava is five steps ahead and turns around. "Ben, six foot one, wild hair, just had coffee with us."

I want to jump and hug her, or break into a song, or do something. The butterflies in my stomach are back, and they're out of control.

Carl, a retired policeman, now dog rescue volunteer, hands each of us an apron and a couple of gloves. He shows us to the supply closet and goes over the order in which the cabins need to be cleaned before a new animal can move in. They look like vacation rentals, except for the tiled walls.

"Hose it down, wipe it dry. Take a new rag for each cabin. The sanitizing spray is in the room I just showed you. Any questions?"

It sounds as if we've just been read our rights.

"I'm helping the guys fix the fence down there, in case you need me." Carl grabs his toolbelt and off he goes.

Ava's last sentence plays in my head like a looped jingle. "My brother."

"You sure look happy," Rita says as she puts on the rubber gloves.

"Ava is Ben's sister." I try to keep my voice down, but it still comes out too loud.

"I know."

"I thought they were a couple, didn't you?"

"No, not really."

All of my pent-up energy goes into mopping the floor.

"That's why you're in no hurry to leave now, I understand," Rita says with a smile and turns off the hose. "He's an awfully nice young man."

Crazy cute he is. And those eyes. I do a mental wardrobe check and want to kick myself for only bringing yoga pants, the baggy kind. I haven't done yoga in years.

"What a lovely place they've built here," Rita says.

It makes total sense to wear comfortable travel clothes. Max and his stupid comments on how I dress. He's so superficial.

"... spending their lives helping dogs."

I wish I'd packed something pretty.

We move on to the next kennel and I ask Rita how long she's planning to stay in Vegas.

"Depends," she says.

"Don't you think I deserve a little more than that?"

"It depends on a few personal matters I have to attend to."

Our eyes briefly meet before she turns her attention back to the floor. I thought I had her figured out by now. Dog-loving widow on memory lane, likes gambling and free drinks, and carries the cremated remains of her husband wherever she goes. Except now, she's without her bag for the first time. Frank was probably no fan of cleaning, either.

The phone vibrates in my pocket, but by the time I dry off my hands, it stops.

"Okay, Paula, here's the thing."

Oh no, please don't let it be another dead body.

"Half of the story you already know. I want Frank to come home."

I wish I hadn't asked.

"The other part is that I mean it literally."

"Huh?"

"We're moving back into our house." She folds her arms in front of her chest and smiles victoriously. "The home we shared for forty-two years."

"And why didn't we go to that place right away?" I ask.

Rita chews on her lip.

"What is it? Can you be straightforward with me for once? I have no more patience for your mysterious hints. Just say it, Rita."

"It's crazy Lola. She lives there."

I try to make sense of all these names and connections. Why would the ex-wife be living in their house?

"When we finally got the diagnosis of Frank's illness, they said a different climate might be good for him. We left for the coast within a week, and a friend of ours offered to help with the sale of our home. He had just gotten divorced, you know. We were glad that the house wouldn't be empty, and he needed a place to stay.

"In the beginning he would call every week, let us know if there was a showing and what the realtor had said. Then the phone calls got less, and one day a moving van with all our furniture appeared out of nowhere. Frank's health was declining, and I had bigger things to worry about. Long story short, Lola had gotten wind of our hasty departure and the arrangement with our friend. She hooked up with him and the next thing we knew she had moved into our house."

"Seriously?"

"She was an attractive woman and always got what she wanted."

"But you must have all the documents with your name on title. Did you ever try to get it back?"

"The first year after Frank's passing, I couldn't care less. Just made it through a day at a time."

My phone vibrates again. Unknown number. I send it to voicemail.

"At some point I paid a lawyer in Sacramento to look into it. Recommended by my landlord. By the time I realized what a useless guy he was, I had paid him five thousand dollars and was not one step further. Then my brother died and left me the place I now live in, plus some cash. A few months ago, I got a letter from our so-called friend. He now lives in a mobile home park in Arizona. He wrote to say how sorry he was about everything that happened. Apparently, he'd tried to come clean with me a couple of times, but Lola would block every attempt. He moved out last year. The letter also contained a newspaper clipping and the last utility bill in his name. He said that I should go after her, and he asked me to forgive him."

Rita looks so fragile as she leans against the wall.

"Did he offer to help you, or at least be a witness?"

"No address on the envelope."

"What was the article about?"

"Squatters in Nevada."

"And what's your plan?"

"I'm done with lawyers, there must be a better way. Look"—she pulls up her necklace and shows me a brass key—"I can still get in."

"If your story's true, I'm sure they would've changed the lock."

"You think I'm lying?"

"So far, you've come up with a new story a day, or if you like to call it, a new element to your story. I honestly don't know what to think anymore."

"I swear, Paula, this is it. You know everything now."

"But where do you start? Didn't you plan anything?"

"Not really." She smiles. "But look how far I've come."

"Still busy?" Ben says, leaning against the doorframe of the supply room. "I almost feel bad for keeping you, but then again, not really."

The butterflies inside start dancing again, and every inch of my skin is tingling.

"We just moved Luna into her new room. They're all doing well."

Our eyes meet and this time I hold his gaze.

"Also, Adam just got home, and he would love to see the bass, if you don't mind."

"Is he a musician?" My hands look for something to do, so I pick up the hose from the ground and look at the nozzle.

"Among other things, yes."

"What does he play?"

"Anything you put in his hands, you'll see. His room is at the far end."

I switch the setting from jet to cone to angular. I must have pushed a little too hard and water shoots out and up the ceiling. I look at Rita, drying my hand on my jeans.

"I'll be fine, Paula. We're almost done here anyway."

"Let's clean up together," Ben says to Rita and takes the dripping hose from my hands. "I'm sure you didn't come to Vegas to clean kennels."

No, I want to shout, she came to bury her dead husband in someone else's yard.

CHAPTER Fifteen

"**He told you** about my teeth, didn't he?" Adam says as he throws a heap of clothes from the couch onto his bed. I tried not to stare at his mouth when he opened the door, but he noticed anyway.

"See? As good as new." He parts his lips and reveals a perfect row of white teeth, the shiniest thing I can spot in the room.

There are so many guitars on the wall it looks like a museum, an electric piano as a room divider, and a drum set in the corner. Part music studio, part computer lab, piles of magazines so high that there's no need for curtains, and a collection of used dishes spread all over the floor. This is either the making of a creative genius or a total dump. Adam himself looks as if he never sees the light of day. His pale skin is framed by even paler hair which sticks out at all sides.

"So, where did you get it and why are you driving it halfway across the country?"

"A friend of mine sold it to a collector from L.A., and I'm just the courier."

"May I?" He takes the instrument from my hands and opens the zipper with the tenderness of a first-time lover.

"Are you fucking kidding me?" He practically hyperventilates. "A Prescott?"

And I thought Max was intense.

"What's the big deal with it?"

He looks at me, part pity, part contempt, and leans the bass against the wall.

"See all these?" He points at the wall of guitar art.

I'm counting nine. He takes down a blue one and throws it in my direction. I jump and barely make the catch. The unexpected weight makes me stumble backward and land on the couch.

"My first bass—bought it used at Steve's Strings in Jersey City. Are you okay?"

I nod and try to look as if I know what I'm doing. My hands are too small. Neck on the right or left? I see Paul McCartney on one of the magazine covers on the floor and I do what he does.

"You're a lefty, too?" he asks.

"Huh?"

"Do you play left-handed, like Paul?"

"I've never played anything." I turn the thing around and Adam puts the strap over my head.

"Go ahead, just try it. I want you to know what a cheap instrument feels like."

I look down at the strings and carefully pull one with my index finger.

"Not a rocker, are you? You're holding it like a wet towel."

I never hung out with the cool kids in school. Maybe I could tell a guitar from a bass if I'd dated a guy like Drew Melnik. Maybe I'd even know how to ride a motorbike.

"Go a little harder, it won't bite you."

Or maybe I would have been busted for Melnik's illegal grow and done community service while pregnant like his girlfriend Cookie, who's now his ex-wife and runs a daycare in her mother's basement.

Pling, pling, pling.

"Hey, not bad. I wouldn't call you a natural, but you get the idea."

It hurts like hell, I'm definitely not a string person.

"Now look at this one, vintage Fender."

He pulls a case from underneath the couch and takes out a cherry-red bass guitar.

"What do you think, not bad, huh?"

He strums a chord. "Paid twelve grand for this baby. She's from the sixties. Here, try her."

He puts the Fender in my lap, seemingly unaware that I'm still holding on to guitar number one which is now squeezed tightly against my chest. Pling, pling. Feels like the other one. Just like the pain.

"Whole new world, isn't it?"

The color's nice.

"If these were cars, the first one'd be a five-hundred-dollar junker. The Fender on the other hand," he looks up as if the answer was written on the ceiling, "MG convertible."

Then he goes back to my bass and puts one arm around it.

"This one here," he glides his hand up and down its neck, "Bentley Continental. With Esperanza in the driver's seat."

"Who?"

"Esperanza Spalding. Hottest bassist on the planet."

He would really hit it off with Max.

He inspects the bass bag and puts his finger through the tear from the Tahoe door handle.

"What's this?" he asks. "Don't tell me you drove her here without a hard case?"

I shrug.

"Where're you from again?"

"Vancouver."

"Canada?"

I nod.

"You drove down the coast, through the mountains, into the desert in like, a week or so?"

"Yes."

"Humidifier?"

"Nope."

"In a fucking canvas bag?"

"Uh-huh."

He sits down on a heap of String Magazine and buries his face in his hands. After a lot of head shaking and eye rubbing, he looks at me with an empty expression.

"I'm going to tell you something," he says and lowers his voice. "If it was up to me, we'd be saving instruments, not dogs."

He leans back with the confidence of someone who's just come up with the formula for world peace.

"Are you serious?"

"Nah, dogs are all right." He grins.

My arm's getting numb. "Would you mind?" I hand the red one back to him and he puts it back in its case.

"Still, instruments have souls, too. Just listen to this baby."

He points at the Prescott's shiny back, takes a bow from behind the couch and starts playing.

"Perfection," he says. The sound is warm and low. "It was built in the eighteen forties, in New Hampshire. From the single most delicate wood Abraham Prescott was able to find."

He keeps playing with his eyes closed.

"She probably had a pretty good life when she was young. Found herself a nice guy, steady gig, New York Phil maybe. Someone took good care of her. Then, for whatever reason, she ends up in Canada, no offence. And now we have two issues. One—old, and two—thin. In wood world that means, stay away from Las Vegas."

In human world it's Rita.

"And how much is it worth?"

He stops playing. "Fifty grand."

"What?"

"Maybe more." He pulls on his earlobe. "At least before the trip."

My stomach cramps up.

"Did I wreck it?"

"Hard to say. I can check for cracks, if you like."

I can't believe Max didn't tell me any of this. Fifty thousand dollars.

"Now, don't feel too bad. If the idiot who bought it didn't organize for professional delivery, that's his fault."

Maybe he did, but the idiot who sent me to do the job wanted to make the extra money.

"What should I do now?"

"Leave her with me for the night. I've got humidifiers."

Leave the fancy bass here, with a stranger? I should call Max. Then again, he hasn't been helpful at all. I try to read Adam's face. Big curious eyes, like a kid. He's polite, and he smiles a lot. Sure, the room's a mess, and his demeanor a bit eccentric. That doesn't mean he'd run off with my bass and sell it. Or would he?

"Adam," I start in a light tone. "Don't take this the wrong way, but I think it should stay with me for the night."

"Okay." He swipes some crumbs off a music stand.

I want to trust him, but I've already made so many mistakes on this trip.

"Honestly, Adam, I don't know anything about you, and it's not even my bass."

"Ask Ava and Ben, they know me well."

Both of whom I only met this morning.

"And what makes you an expert in instruments? Apart from the fact that you've got humidifiers, obviously."

"If it helps, this is me up there."

He points at a blown-up photo on the wall. Six guys in tuxedos posing in front of a grand piano. I hardly recognize him because of the tan, and the adult hair.

"I'm a cellist. Performance degree from Juilliard, the whole bit."

He waves at some framed awards.

"Played with the Pittsburgh Symphony for a season, then this cruise ship gig."

"Great picture."

"Yeah, luckily you can't see the fucked-up singer we had to accompany every night."

"Sounds like fun to travel the world for work."

"It wears off." He leafs through a pile of papers that he's pulled from underneath a dinner plate. "The criminal record check from that gig must be here somewhere."

"Did you move to Vegas from there?"

"Yeah, they offered me a gig at Circus Circus, playing chamber music in a clown costume. It was either that, or Les Misérables on tour, you know, rooming with a drunk drummer at some Days Inn. No thanks."

I look around and realize that one wall is covered in newspaper clippings, framed photographs, awards. Adam with an orchestra, Adam in a studio, Adam at Disneyland, Adam smiling with a cello in his arm.

"I walked from the music business, but I still know my shit."

"Will you be here tomorrow morning?"

"You bet. This is my office."

From the same plate-holding paper pile, he produces a business card: Adam McGhee * TechnoNurse * Steps from the Strip * On-site Visits.

I look at his baby face and back at the card. "What exactly is your job?"

"Stripper."

"Seriously?"

"No," he laughs. "Computer nerd. Hardware, software, web design."

I wash my hands in the RV sink and catch a glance in the mirror. The eyeliner I'd thrown on at dawn lines everything but my eye, and the mascara has migrated to a place that doesn't even have lashes. My hair looks like seaweed, and there's only one earring. A birthday gift from Julian. I pat down my shirt in search of the missing one, but it's gone.

I rub the black smudge from my face, search the drawer for a hair tie, and dab on a drop from a perfume sample on my neck and wrist, Calvin Klein *Eternity*. It smells way too strong and I start rubbing it off when I see Ben outside. He's walking with the antenna-eared dogs and is just steps away from the RV. I open the door and play surprised.

"Oh, hi. How are they doing?"

"Quite fearful, they'll need to learn to trust again."

I step outside which startles the dogs and they both start barking.

"Would you like to join us for a walk?" Ben asks.

His voice calms me and I feel that my brain is finally working again.

"Actually, I have plans to take Rita into town. Sort of a girls' night out."

"Sounds good. If you're not too tired and want to hang out with some locals, just come in through the courtyard. We'll be up late, I'm sure."

"Thanks, maybe I will."

"Also, RV parking's illegal in Vegas, take my car." He pulls a Volvo key from his pocket. "The white station wagon over there. No AC, but the sunroof works."

His hand brushes against mine when he hands me the key.

"Thank you, I don't know, that's very nice of you, I—"

"Have fun and see you later."

He turns to leave, and the car keys in my hand have reached melting temperature. So has my heart.

"Paula, why don't you answer your phone? I'm about to freak out." Max catches me on the cell just as Rita and I are getting into the car.

"Everything's gone sideways. That stupid space-cat wife is back with her husband, all lovey dovey. They're making up in the Caymans, talking babies and stuff. I need the bass back ASAP or else my buddy will go to hell."

"The drummer she ran off with?"

"Yeah, the boho life wasn't for her. Where are you now?"

"Still in Vegas."

"You need to get behind the wheel now."

"No."

"My buddy's scared shitless, Paula."

"Your buddy's a moron."

"He hasn't been back to his place, threatens to stay with me until this is resolved. Apparently, the rich fart knows some heavies."

"Max?"

"Yes."

"I'm not driving back today."

Silence.

"I've been on the road for fourteen hundred miles. I'm exhausted, I need to shower, I want to see Vegas and the stupid bass is always in the way. And, on top of everything else, this thing is worth more than I've ever seen in my life. Adam says only an idiot would drive a Prescott through the desert."

"Who's Adam, and why does he care?"

"He's the friend of the guy who helped me with the dog. Long story. But he knows everything about instruments and gave me this whole lecture. Anyway, the bass is with him for the night and if you need it now, you'll have to get it yourself."

"But Paula, I don't understand, what's the difference? If I hadn't called, you'd be on your way to L.A., so just drive home instead."

It's not often that Max sounds stressed. He does now.

"Aren't you in a hurry to save your job?"

My job. I haven't thought about it all day. This deal here might be the only income I can count on for a while. Will Max even pay me if he can't sell the bass?

"Now that I know about the damn thing, I can't strap fifty thousand uninsured dollars back in the camper and sleep at Walmart. And, if you must know, an old lady needs my help, too, and she means a lot to me."

And then there's Ben, but I keep that to myself.

"How about we meet halfway?" Max asks.

"Will you still pay me?"

I hear his fingers tap on the phone before he says, "Portland, tomorrow night."

"Forget it."

His tapping gets faster. "Okay, Portland on Monday, I'll pay you half."

"San Francisco and I'll keep it all."

"When did you become so badass?"

"Twenty years too late."

CHAPTER Sixteen

From the distance Las Vegas looks like any other big city. Futuristic high-rises held together by strings of freeways. We take the downtown exit, and the streets get narrow. Every traffic light is red, which gives me time to look around.

"This is the old part," Rita says. "Some of the original casinos are still standing, like the Golden Nugget over there. It's fun to come here at night. The street performers are really something else, and gambling is cheaper, too." She looks at her watch. "It's a bit early now."

"Can you walk to the Strip from here?"

"It would be quite a walk, with some sketchy neighborhoods along the way," she says.

Hordes of tourists in flip flops ramble along the streets. Some of them wear shirts with suggestive messages, guaranteed to vanish in the back of the closet once they're back home in Boise or Buffalo. There's a sunburned Elvis, holding a bottle in one hand and a giggly girl in the other. They're struggling to walk straight as they follow her selfie stick. Even though our light has switched to green, the stream of fun seekers keeps moving. Eventually I honk the horn. A staggering guy in his twenties jumps and spills a beer over his chest. He gives me the finger and yells some profanity. In the mirror I see him trying to hit us with the empty can.

It's boiling hot and I'm starting to envy the crowd outside for their summer outfits. I roll down the window with a handle, eighties style.

"Turn right at the next light," Rita says.

One side of the road is lined with wedding chapels.

"This is where you get married Vegas-style."

They're smaller than I imagined. Graceland Wedding Chapel, Cupids Wedding Chapel, a drive-thru window, and a 50% off special (Monday through Wednesday, 8-10 AM)

The next one I've seen on TV shows. I think Rachel and Ross got married there.

"The Little White Chapel," Rita says and points to the left. "It's my favorite."

"Did you marry Frank here?"

She nods. "It was quieter then."

Traffic's moving slowly. We pass a pawn shop, a barber, and a weed dispensary. A broken sign for payday loans flickers randomly.

"How far are we from your house, Rita?"

She doesn't react.

"Seriously, you've been telling me all these stories, we're here now and I'd like to see it."

She bites her lip and rubs Toto so vigorously that he jumps off her lap.

"That's what you came for, Rita. Please, show me the way."

"I'm not ready." She looks the other way. "It's too soon."

I hit the brakes hard and pull to the side.

"That's the lamest excuse and you know it."

She takes a deep breath.

"I'm scared, Paula."

"We're going."

The last thing I expect after the rundown rentals with barred windows is a neighborhood like Paradise Palms. I feel as if I've been sucked into a time machine and spit out into sixties suburbia. Every bungalow has its own personality, every front yard a story to tell. Some homes have been renovated and enjoy their second spring in a turquoise or lime. Others age quietly without a facelift.

"It's beautiful, Rita. I'd move here in a second."

"Isn't it? I was afraid my memory made it grander over the years."

She turns her head from left to right as we drive along. "Wait, take the next left and then down one block."

I follow her directions until she motions me to slow down.

"That's it, there's our house."

I make a U-turn and park the car between two SUVs. It's not one of the flashy houses, even though the butterfly roof makes it stand out from its neighbors. I try to picture the faded pink with a fresh coat of paint. The creeping roots from a tree that looks a hundred years old push through the concrete driveway.

"Maybe that's her car." I point at the baby blue pickup parked on the curve. Missing hub caps and a dented side.

"Maybe it is."

I turn off the engine.

"Now, how are you planning to get your house back?"

"It was a bad idea to come here. Let's forget it and go for coffee."

She lowers the sun visor and pulls on her seatbelt.

"*Now* you want to give up? You swirl into my life, derail every one of my plans, and suddenly it's a bad idea?"

Rita blows her nose.

"We're not going anywhere." I unbuckle my seatbelt and lower the backrest. "I can sit here all night, so you'd better come up with a plan."

"I haven't thought it through," Rita says, staring at the house. "I don't know what I was thinking, I'm sorry. Let's go and do something fun, shall we?"

Only yesterday I would have agreed, happy to get on with my life.

"What did Lola look like when you last saw her?"

"Tall, slender, auburn hair. Always dressed in black."

"I could go up to the house and pretend to be looking for someone. Let's at least find out if she still lives here."

"I don't know."

"You wait here, no matter what, okay?"

Without waiting for an answer, I get out of the car, cross the street, and ring the doorbell. Nothing happens. Through the frosted glass I see the reflection of a TV set flickering. I hit the bell again and wait for a few minutes. As I turn around to leave, a woman around forty, maybe younger, opens the door just enough for her head to fit through. She stares at me with puffy eyes.

"Hi," I say and produce a trustworthy smile.

She yawns. Judging by her collapsed beehive, she just woke up. She wears a sports bra and boxer shorts, three sizes too small. Both of them. I almost forget my line.

"I hope I didn't interrupt anything important, but I'm looking for my dog. About this size, black and white, curly tail. He took off at the end of the cul-de-sac, and I thought I saw him running into your yard."

"Nope, nothing here." She suppresses another yawn.

"Wait, maybe he ran into the backyard. Do you mind taking a quick look for me?"

"I'm busy."

She's about to close the door.

"Maybe I could drop by later?" I move in closer. "I swear I saw little Poochie run this way."

"Then I hope he takes off before my aunt gets home. She knows how to deal with them flea bags."

I try to peek inside, but it's too dark. "This is your aunt's house?"

"None of your business."

She slams the door and misses my face by an inch. I start walking toward the Volvo but decide against it in case she's watching from behind the window. I look around. The house next door with its manicured lawn and angel sculptures looks more inviting. A gentleman in pressed jeans and a wide smile opens the door on the second ring. His teeth are whiter than his hair.

"Good afternoon, Mr.—," I glance at the brass plate below the doorbell. "Mr. Stederman, I'm sorry to bother you. My husband and I are looking to buy a place a couple of houses down from yours, and I'm wondering if it really is as quiet as the agent is telling us."

The shiny smile freezes. Maybe he hasn't heard me. Then he turns around and yells into the house. "Is Fred moving out after all?"

He faces me again. "That son of a bitch. Wouldn't give it to my boy when he offered him way over market value."

A woman his age with puffed-up hair appears behind him. She's carrying a Pekingese and wears the kind of satiny slippers that died along with nylon house robes and cigarette holders. She looks me up and down. My travel gear can't compete with her pant suit.

"This young lady wants to move here, asking about our street."

"Well, we're actually looking at a house in the street behind you. I believe the backyard would be facing your neighbor's house."

I point in the general direction I came from.

The wife puts one finger to her lip. "Who would that be I wonder? The Packeltons maybe?"

"I bet it's Fred, that spineless crook. Won't admit that it's time for assisted living."

Their idle talk gives me time to fluff up my story.

"The thing is, my husband would only consider buying if there were no kids or barking dogs in the neighborhood. He's very prone to headaches."

I married an uptight jerk who hates kids and sends his bride to spy on the neighbors.

"Is that a quiet household over there?" I point over to Lola's, hiding my ringless hand from the Stedermans. My husband's also too cheap for diamonds.

Fred looks at his wife and hesitates before he answers.

"We don't socialize with those people."

"Trash," she whispers.

"Actually, it's just the woman living there now," Fred continues. "Don't know what happened to the fellow. He seemed nice enough. What was his name again?"

"She's so—I want to say—vulgar." Mrs. Stederman covers her mouth with one hand. "When we bought the house, I went over to introduce myself. She was drinking out of the can. And when she saw little Monty here, she just about slammed the door in my face."

She kisses the panting dog on the nose. "She was afraid of my little baby, yes she was. Who's the best doggie in the world? Who is it?"

I think we all know who it is.

"Has she always lived here?" I ask Mr. Stederman and point at Lola's house.

"Well—" he clears his throat.

"She's been here since we bought the house," his wife cuts in. "We were over on Ottawa Drive before we built the house. But my husband kept missing the steps to the sunken living room, so we sold."

"It was the carpet," he says. "Happened to you, too."

She pushes him aside and gets closer to my face.

"The couple in the white house over there, with the tall hedge, they shoot movies by the pool, if you know what I mean."

She lowers her voice. "Sometimes they have other couples over. We only hear the music."

"Barry White," her husband says.

"They play the same thing over and over. But we don't see anything. The hedge is tall.

"Very tall," he says.

"You've both been most helpful. It certainly seems to be a peaceful part of town."

"It's paradise. You and your husband must come over for drinks if you decide to buy."

I'm sure my husband wouldn't go with his migraines and all the sex talk.

CHAPTER Seventeen

We're sitting at the Paris, at last, sipping café au lait from French coffee bowls. Rita wants to know every detail of my encounter with Lola's niece and the neighbors.

"Just think of the cream-colored Stedermans with Lola on one side and an adult-movie set on the other."

"Another thing they don't have at Golden Pond."

I take one of the pastries from the tray in front of me.

"What do we do now?"

Rita looks at her watch. "First we'll go shopping, and then depending on how we're doing with time, I can show you around Fremont Street."

"I'm talking about your house."

I take a big bit. The cream filling bursts out of the éclair and onto my sweater.

"Paula, dear, you look a little, shall we say, ruffled. With the dog hair, and the stains."

"Just a bit of hot water and you won't even see it."

"But I want to do something nice for you, you've helped me so much."

"Please don't take me shopping, I hate it."

"We'll make it fun," she says.

I've heard that before, never worked.

"Ben is awfully charming, don't you think? And so handsome. I've noticed the way he looks at you."

"It doesn't matter how he looks at me. I live in Canada, Rita, twelve hundred miles away."

"So what? A little fling won't hurt anyone. And if nothing happens, at least you'll go back home with new clothes."

I let the last piece of coffee-drenched pastry melt on my tongue. Rita sticks her hand inside her rolled-up jacket. Toto's been hiding in there, quiet as a mouse. But just as the server passes by, he lets out a shrill bark.

She wipes our table and points at the coat. "You're not allowed to bring pets. May I ask you to take the dog outside, please?"

Rita uncovers Toto's face and shakes her head.

"He's an emotional support animal, would you like to see the papers?"

The waitress stares Rita down in a way that says, 'we both know that's a lie,' then she leaves.

I'm in the dressing room at a hip little store, squeezing my legs into a pair of very skinny jeans. I've already collected a pile of *yes* clothes and hung the *don't knows* over the door. Maybe it's the vibe of the city, but I find this shopping spree more enjoyable than my dreaded trips to a mall. I try on the red dress that Rita's added to the pile. When I step out to have a look in the mirror, the sales assistant says between two bubbles of her gum, "Honey, you're born to wear that dress, and we don't work on commission."

"Really?"

"Uh-huh."

"Don't you think it's a bit tight around here?"

Her pointy nails dig into my waist, pull on the fabric, and let it bounce back.

"Two percent Lycra. Fits better than your own skin."

I look around for Rita.

"Have you seen the lady who was here just a minute ago?" I ask the sales assistant.

"She's in here, I made her try a few things."

The curtain opens and Rita steps out in a sixties-looking wrap dress. Shiny earrings are dangling every time she moves, and Toto peeks out of a faux fur backpack.

"Now, shoes. Follow me this way, girlfriends."

When we leave the store, the assistant hugs us goodbye and insists we see her stylist at Live and Let Dye. She also makes me wear the high heels I bought and stuffs my old clothes in a bag.

The sidewalk is packed, dance music pounding from the outdoor speakers. We meander around the party people and by the time we reach the salon, nine of my toes are numb. I limp past the reception desk and plop down in a chair that looks like a giant egg cut in half. Rita crawls into another one.

"How's it going?" the receptionist asks. She's in a silver jumpsuit, her braids pointing up like antennae.

I explain that the salon was recommended to me and that I don't have an appointment. She checks the screen, then talks into her headset.

"It'll just be a few minutes. Would you like the goggles?"

I don't know what she means.

"For the VR feature in the relaxation pod?" She points at the egg I sit in. "Space Odyssey, Cat Purr, or Zen Garden."

"Space Odyssey, please," Rita says and sinks back into the chill pod.

I haven't even had time to switch into runners when the receptionist lets me know that SheeVonn, junior PhD—professional hair dramaturge—has a cancellation and is willing to take me on.

"Hi gorgeous, my name is Vonn. SheeVonn." He pulls a brush from his holster like a handgun. "How can I further enhance your beauty today?"

I release my hair from the ponytail.

"Hmm," he walks around me, chin resting in his hand.

"Yes, we can do something with that, we definitely can."

He circles me again, rubs at a spot on my scalp, parts my hair in the back, twists it into a bun, tousles it with a brush and lets it all go.

"I don't style, I transform. I did an *American Idol* contestant, I did Jennifer, I'd do Elton if he ever comes back. Now, where do we start?"

The name-dropping makes me nervous. They don't do that at Great Clips.

"Just a basic wash and style, thanks."

"Just wash and style? This ain't your strip mall barber, honey. We texturize, we volumize, we glamorize. We don't do *just*."

He blows into his brush-pistol and puts it back in his holster.

"I, um, I don't know. I really only need shampoo."

He looks concerned as he glides his hand through my hair again.

"Your ends are drier than Death Valley in June. Why do you hate your hair?"

The woman with the tin-foiled head in the next chair throws me a contemptuous look. SheeVonn says the only way to turn this straw into gold is with a dusting trim and a prickly pear mask. It sounds expensive.

"Your coloring is nice, actually. Picture all this in shiny, a few highlights around your face, not too much. I'm thinking sun-kissed toffee. You'll love it."

This guy worked on one of the Jennifers, and he likes my hair color?

"Okay," I hear myself say. "Do this toffee thing."

He says he'll throw in a toner for free.

"What can I get you while you wait? Manhattan? Mojito?"

"Just juice, please. No ice."

My PhD returns with a drink which, he assures me, "Is basically virgin with just a naughty splash."

SheeVonn wraps a cutting cape around my shoulders and gets to work. The drink tastes like strawberries and chocolate. And when I lift my feet just one inch off the floor, I barely feel the pain.

After the nurturing and toning is done, the shine locked in and the frizz combed out, my hair is being wrapped around large rollers by SheeVonn's assistant. She doesn't talk much, but she's really nice to my hair. If I had a boyfriend, I'd want him to do what she does.

My time under the dryer is up and the master's back. He kneads my hair, scrunches here and pulls there, until he leans back and crosses his arms.

"We did it, you look stunning. I like a good challenge."

And I love what he did.

"All we need now is a dash of pearl-infused argan oil with ylang-ylang. Smoothness factor, through the roof."

He dabs a bit on my ends. "Jennifer adores it."

"Which Jennifer?"

He looks at the receptionist and back at me.

"You're hilarious. Don't you read *InStyle* up north?"

He slides a tiny bottle into my hand, and the receptionist announces the grand total for today's transformation. I almost faint and toss the oil back at SheeVonn. My car cost less.

"Don't panic, you'll only need two drops," he says. "It'll last you forever."

So does the Corolla.

The street is as packed as it was before, but nobody bumps into me. People are dancing on the sidewalk, a couple kissing intimately as if they were the only two people in the world. Ben's face pops up in my head. I bet he's a good kisser.

"Paula, wasn't the parking garage the other way?" Rita points in the direction we came from.

She's right. We turn and walk back. Another two blocks in these heels, but my toes don't burn anymore. The two lovers are still lost in a kiss. I just smiled at someone for no reason.

"We can't be too far from your old neighborhood. Should we see if Lola's home?" I ask Rita as we get into the car.

"She might spoil your mood," she says.

"Impossible." I throw the bags on the backseat and buckle in. "Vegas likes me."

By the time we get to Seneca Drive, Rita's more awake. I stop the car on a dark stretch of the street where we have a good view of the house. The Chevy's gone, but somebody's home. The front window is half-covered by a curtain and there's a shadow moving from one side of the room to the other.

"That's the kitchen," Rita says. "I wish I could just walk right in and throw her out."

We sit in silence and watch the shadow move around Rita's life.

"You have the key with you, right?"

She nods.

"Okay, here's the plan. As soon as she settles in another room, we'll quietly go and try the key. No turning, just check if it fits. Then you go back to the car and watch while I ring the bell and involve her in some chitchat."

Rita wrinkles her forehead. "Why would we do that?"

"We need to make sure that it's her, and that the lock's still the same. Which will then be further proof that your story's true."

"You still don't believe me?"

"I do, but the police may get involved."

She rests her head against the window and sighs.

"This is your house, Rita, and we'll take it back. I promise."

We're about to cross the street when I notice Toto huddled in Rita's arm.

"Why him?" I whisper and point at the dog.

"Emotional support," she says and clutches him a little closer.

We sneak up the driveway, careful not to kick a pebble and disturb the silence. By the time we reach the front door, my heartbeat is the only sound I hear. Rita gives me the key.

"Here, you do it. My hands are shaking."

We both squeeze into the corner of the entrance way and I slide the key into the lock and turn it ever so slightly. It fits. Hard to believe that no one's ever changed the lock in all these years. I'd like to see Rita's smile now. Instead, she pounds on my back like a butcher on dead meat. I look up and see a shadow at the other side of the glass. Oh no, not now. Why did I have to turn the key? Now it's stuck. The shadow's getting taller. It needs to come out fast, or else we're in trouble.

"Who's there?"

I jump back and let go of the key. The lights go on and the door opens a crack. A woman with bright lipstick pokes her head out and starts to yell, but when she sees Rita the words die on her lips.

"You don't believe in telephones?" she says and takes a puff from her cigarette. She's taller than I am, and skinnier, too. Even with her baked skin she's an attractive woman.

"So, you went blond," Rita says.

"What do you want here? Tired of bore town?" Lola shoots back.

"Catch a show, shop a little, the usual. Thought you'd never forgive me if I didn't say hello."

"Hi and bye." She tries to bang the door, but Rita has her foot in the frame.

"Leeching season's over, Lola. We can do it civilized and you can leave quietly, or my lawyer is going to kick you out, your choice."

"Ooh, I'm so scared of your big lawyer." She grimaces, waving her pointy fingernails in Rita's face. "Tell the idiot to stop filling my garbage with his mail."

"Why don't you tell that to my new lawyer?" Rita says and puts her hand on my arm. "She's right here."

Both women look at me with great expectation.

"That true?" Lola asks, looking me up and down.

"Why wouldn't it?"

"Better get yourself a nice pant suit, Barbie."

I step up to her eye level.

"What I wear or don't wear is none of your business. You're out of here by noon tomorrow."

I force her to keep eye contact so that she doesn't see the key is still stuck. "I can also send my guys over, if that'll get you moving a little faster."

She yells at us to back off or else she'll call the cops.

"And tell them what?" I ask. "That the lawful owner is back to kick you out? They'll be glad to help."

"Get the hell out of here. I've got better things to do."

Toto, who's been rolled up in Rita's arm until now, jumps up and starts to bark. He stares at Lola, shaking and showing his tiny teeth.

"Get that thing away from me," Lola screams. She takes a step back and starts coughing. "Are you trying to kill me? Go away."

She bends over and holds on to the wall as the coughing takes hold of her. I grab the door with one hand and wiggle the key out of the lock.

"You'd better start packing." I pull Rita by the sleeve, as the lights go on in the house next door. We scurry across the lawn and I hear Lola slam the door.

"That was the most fun I've had in years," Rita says when we're in the car. "You were great."

"I've never yelled at a stranger in my life."

"Lola sure knows how to press buttons."

She feeds Toto a treat. "This little angel is my hero. Did you see how scared she was of him? Wish I'd known that years ago."

"It's not too late, Rita."

CHAPTER Eighteen

Rita gets ready for bed as soon as we're back and I'm tempted to do the same. The excitement of our adventure has waned, and so has my courage.

"Take Ben up on his invitation. You can sleep when you're dead," she says as she sees me plunge onto the couch. "Go have fun on your first night here."

"I had lots of fun."

"Me too, but you know what I mean. You said it yourself, Vegas likes you."

"I don't know, it's late."

"You don't need to know anything, just live."

I picture Ben and his killer smile.

"I feel like a stranger in this dress."

"You can be whoever you want to be, Paula."

I put on my old sneakers and hug her. "Thank you, Rita."

I follow the path from the parking lot and hear music as I get closer to the house. They're all in the living room. Ava is stretched out under a blanket on one side of the couch, the giant dog covers the rest. Adam has folded himself into a burgundy armchair. Ben and another guy sit cross-legged in front of the fireplace. I knock and Ben jumps up to let me in.

"Hi Paula, come in. We've just opened a nice red."

Ava's dog leaves the couch with a sigh, and I sit down in his place.

"He's so well-mannered," Ava says. "Guys could learn from him."

"You've got to lower your expectations," Adam says without looking up from his magazine. "You know that the perfect man's right here." He points at his chest. "Whenever you're ready."

He flips another page of *Downbeat. Jazz, Blues & Beyond.*

"Thanks, I'll stay with the dog," Ava says.

Ben hands me a glass of wine.

"You haven't met Xavier yet, the genius who found us this place. Xavier, this is Paula. I told you about my trip to the shelter this morning."

"Nice to meet you."

We shake hands.

"This is the most beautiful house I've ever seen."

"You should have seen it before," Ava says. "It was nothing like this. But Xavier had this vision, and nothing could stop him. He's our artist in residence. A modest one, though."

She smiles at him.

"We're a good team," he says.

Ben raises his glass. "To Noah's Bark. International, cross-species utopian commune."

"No, man, not again." Adam looks up from his magazine.

"He doesn't like labels," Ben says and sits beside me on the couch.

"Just leave me alone with politics and shit. I'm not a goody good doer."

"What are you then?" Ava asks.

"I live here with my friends and a pack of dogs. End of story."

Ben leans closer to me. "Adam's a bit traumatized. His parents were real hippies."

"Hey, I heard that."

"He hates the word commune."

"Believe me, you would, too," Adam says. "Sit-ins, love-ins, sharing everything. That crap didn't work then, and it doesn't work now."

He drops the magazine and rubs his eyes. "My parents are so messed up. Why do you think I turned into a computer nerd?"

"Rebellion, we know," Ava says and throws a cracker at him.

"Damn right." He turns toward me. "You know, I was home-schooled by a bunch of potheads, my hair had never been cut, my clothes were genderless. How can you freak out your parents when everything's allowed?"

I wish I'd had his problem growing up.

"At fourteen I moved to New Jersey with my grandparents. First time in public school and I sucked at everything, except band. You know why? Hippie kids grow up in drum circles."

"I thought you studied cello."

"Later, yes. But I got turned on to strings in the commune. One of my mother's boyfriends gave me his sitar. Nine years later it was my ticket into Orchestra One at Edison High."

"Are your parents still there?"

"No, but they're still together believe it or not. Totally mainstream as my mother put it. Whatever that means. I haven't seen them in years."

Ben's knee is so close to mine that I feel the fold of his jeans.

"Ava and Ben's family is the only normal one I know. Seriously, too good to be true. But ask Xavier what he thinks of his padres."

"My father wouldn't say hi to me on the street," Xavier says. "Luckily he's in Guadalajara. I grew up there."

"And lucky for us, he's ours now." Ava blows an air kiss his way. "Without Xavier we wouldn't have Noah's Bark."

"Was it a dog rescue from the start?"

"Not at all. These two guys here were just looking to invest in real estate."

"More like, condo with a pool," Adam says, and Ava rolls her eyes.

"I knew Adam from my work at the animal hospital—he's our computer guy—and Xavier shared a place with my brother at the time. Where did you meet again?"

"First year philosophy," they say in unison. "Critical thinking 101."

"Right. And Xavier convinced us to invest in this handy-man's special."

"So much work," Adam mumbles through a mouthful of peanuts. "A critical thinker should have foreseen that."

"There were six of us originally. One dropped out before the house was finished and the other one, well, utopia and love don't always work out." Ava looks at Ben. He leans back, arms crossed in front of his chest.

"How did you end up with all the dogs then?"

"My boss at the animal hospital is one of the vets who works with the local shelters. At the time we still had a kill shelter in town, which means that every day at five they started euthanizing. My work was at the clinic, but one day Clarke was unavailable, and I had to go."

She pulls the blanket closer.

"I couldn't do it. Just couldn't. I put pets to sleep at our clinic, with the owners there. But this was different. The dogs were brought in first and they knew exactly what was awaiting them as they were dragged across the tiled floor. The girl who worked that day was new. She also had tears in her eyes. I told her that I was taking the dogs with me. 'All nineteen?' she asked. I called the boys and told them to meet me there. Then the girl pointed at the cat kennels piled along the wall and said that they were up next."

"My car smelled for months," Ben says.

"Argh," all three cry out.

"You've whined enough." Ava reaches over me to nudge her brother.

"Adopting five carloads of animals was crazy. We had no kennels, no money, no plan. The only thing in our favor was the fact that this property was originally designed to be a horse farm. That's why there's all this space. Anyway, they gave us a thirty-pound bag of dog food and off we went. Ben's girlfriend at the time was a cat lover. She called everyone she knew and by midnight she'd found foster homes for all but one." Ava leans closer and adds, "Which, by the way, she took with her when she moved out last summer."

"Yadda, yadda, yadda." Ben waves his hands around. "Fast-forward please."

"We worked day and night, built fences, dog runs, and took turns watching the dogs. It was a crazy time. Long story short, we're now officially chartered as a non-profit, donations are tax deductible, the whole bit."

She hugs the sleeping dog. "And this one's my baby, he was the first in line to be put down. Look at his eyes. How could you possibly hurt him? All the other dogs were sent off to new homes, but slobbering St. Bernards are not in fashion, so he's forever mine."

She bends down to kiss his head.

"And then," Adam says, "we learned that we'd struck gold—women stop and talk to you when you're with a dog. Nice women."

"Whatever it takes to get him to help out," Ava says.

"I'd say walking a dog got me more dates than walking the bass. By the way, Paula, your bass plays like a dream. You didn't destroy it on the way down."

"Really?"

"I just found the tiniest crack, but it could have been there before. When do you need it back?"

"I'm leaving Monday."

"Wait, I've only heard some bits and pieces," Ava says. "What exactly brings you to Vegas?"

I start telling the whole story, the missed meeting point, Rita in Tahoe, and how we ended up with Luna. Then I come to the part about Rita's house and tonight's meeting with Lola.

"And judging by her reaction to Toto, she hates dogs. The neighbor said it, too. We're going back tomorrow to hopefully get her out of there."

"I'll come with you, if you like," Ben says. "Maybe with a big dog."

Adam raises his hand. "Count me in, I could use some action."

"I thought you're on Tinder," Xavier says.

"My room's too messy to entertain."

"Clean it up."

"I'm not that desperate."

"No, seriously," Ben says. "If this really is Rita's house, I'm happy to help."

"I've seen the title document. Rita even showed me the restraining order against Lola while they all still lived in Vegas."

"I'm working tomorrow," Ava says. "But I'll send Bear with you. He's big and he drools."

Upon hearing his name, he lifts up his head and stands up. He's the size of a small horse, and when his tongue comes out to wipe over his nose, I feel the spray on my face.

"Just don't use the van, it'll stick out like a sore thumb in Paradise Palms."

"Name one place where it blends in," Adam says.

Ava laughs and gets up. "Goodnight guys, I need to sleep. Been up since five."

"It's been a long day for me, too." I finish the rest of the wine.

"Would you like to say good night to Luna?" Ben asks as he gets up. "Unless you're too tired."

"I would love that."

Why did I have to say 'love'? It sounds way too eager, desperate almost.

"Good," Ben says.

"You guys mind if I play the bass for a bit?" Adam asks.

"Yes," they all yell at the same time.

Xavier curses in Spanish.

"I'll use the tranquilizer dart if I have to," Ava shouts from her room.

Ben opens the patio door. It's even darker now, and a lot colder.

"Listen to the coyotes," Ben says. "They come close once the lights are out."

The howling reminds me of my childhood and all the wild animals we had near our house. What I didn't have then was a ridiculously good-looking man pushing branches out of the way to protect my eyes.

We enter the small room where Rita and I were cleaning bowls earlier in the day. Ben takes a flashlight from the shelf and covers the shine with his hand. Luna lifts her head, and the tip of her tail starts to wag.

"Is it okay to pet her or will it wake up the babies?" I ask Ben.

"I'm not a dog, but a gentle touch would be all right, I think."

I lower to my knees and move my hand forward, careful not to startle her. Luna licks my hand and closes her eyes. I gently knead her ear and she lowers her head back to the ground.

"She trusts you," Ben whispers. He kneels next to me, less than an inch away. I feel the warmth from his body. He smells so good, just like this morning. My legs are starting to numb and I can't feel my right foot, but I don't want this moment to end. He's so close that I feel his breath against my cheek.

"Paula?"

His lips, so close.

"Yes?"

"Let's go back to the house. The floor is very uncomfortable."

What is wrong with me? All day I've told Rita, and myself, that my place is in Vancouver, that I still love Julian. And here I am with Ben and all I want is to kiss him without thinking about the next day.

He puts the flashlight in its spot and locks the door. My heart is hammering in my chest. We walk back the same way we came. While my eyes adjust, Ben takes my hand and guides me through the darkness. Thank you, moon, for hiding behind the cloud until we reach the parking lot.

"Would you like to warm up inside?" he asks, my hand still in his.

The cloud is moving on and I see Ben's face in the moonlight.

"I'm sorry, but—"

"What are you sorry about?"

"I have to go."

I give him a quick kiss on the cheek and turn around.

"Good night, Paula."

"Good night." I keep walking.

"The new dress is stunning, by the way."

My heart's about to explode.

"But you were already perfect without it."

Part of me wants to run after him and shout, *I'd love to warm up with you. I want to kiss you and stay up with you all night and I don't want to drive home yet.* It's the same part which enjoyed trying different clothes, and swimming naked in the hot pool two nights ago.

But the other part sneaks into the RV, undresses in the dark, and wonders what could have been.

I wake up in the middle of the night and can't go back to sleep. Vague images of when I was younger float around in my head, but nothing holds my attention. It's Ben who keeps coming back to my mind. How can I be so attracted to a total stranger? I turn on my phone and google his name. Seven people named Ben Barlow on Facebook, one Ben G. Barlow, and three Benjamins. Two don't have pictures, but their "about" section rules them out. Married, veteran, lives in Alaska. I look up Noah's Bark and find a picture of him. I zoom in on his eyes and stare at them until the butterflies inside make me dizzy.

Just one more day. Be a grown-up, help Rita with her house. Then I'll meet Max in San Francisco and get back to reality.

CHAPTER Nineteen

I **wake up from** the sun stroking my face. What a treat not to bump my head against the edge of the bass first thing in the morning. Rita is talking with someone in the parking lot. I peek out the window and the butterflies return to my belly the second I see Ben.

"If you keep spoiling us like this, we might never leave."

"I'll do my best," he says.

I watch him walk away.

"We just got an invitation for breakfast," Rita says as she steps inside.

"Good, I'll get ready."

"And?"

"And what?"

"How was your evening?" She follows me to the back of the RV.

"Apart from me being grossly overdressed?"

"Apart from that."

"Cold, it was quite cold."

"I'd watch the Weather Channel if I wanted to know the temperature."

"Okay." I shake out the blanket.

"So, did you take my advice? You know, the fling thing?"

"We had a perfectly nice evening, sat by the fire with everybody, had some wine, and then I came back here. End of story."

"Oh." She looks disappointed.

"But I like him a lot. And I mentioned your house being occupied, and guess what, the guys offered to come with us today."

"Really?" she asks.

"I'll tell you everything on the way."

I put on my new pair of jeans and black tee. Hair—less styled, more me. Missed calls—none. I want to embrace the world.

"More coffee anyone?" Xavier asks.

We sit in the courtyard and enjoy a breakfast of granola, blueberries, melons, and croissants. Ben's phone goes off every few minutes, and twice he has to leave the table to talk to possible adopters at the office.

I lean back and turn my face toward the sun. This moment will forever be my happy place. The warmth, the palm trees, the smell of fresh coffee. Everybody's so kind, and we laugh a lot.

"I'd say there's a good chance we can convince Ms. Lola to move out today," Ben says. "We've dealt with some pretty rough dog abusers over the years."

"Ava's like Batman," Adam says. "Remember the dog fighter asshole she took care of? I wonder how long it took for his butt to recover."

"What happened?" I ask.

"Let's just say he'll never tie a dog to his truck again and do donuts," Adam says. "Because, you know, after Ava had to euthanize the dog, she took *him* for a spin."

"Then she remodeled his truck a bit," Xavier adds. "With a hammer."

"Ava did that?"

"Yep," Adam says. "And there were no witnesses."

"Except for us," Xavier says.

"But we didn't see anything." Adam covers his eyes with both hands.

"My sister has a black belt in kung fu and a great lawyer," Ben says. "Although, the lawyer may be out of the picture, after the way she broke up with him."

Rita looks a bit nervous as she shifts in her seat. "I can go the official way and apply for an eviction order."

"Don't worry." Ben puts his arm around her. "Ava's only got a short fuse when she sees animal abuse. We won't tie Lola to a truck."

"We're pretty gentle guys," Xavier says. "It's just that some people, they don't want to listen."

Ben gets up and starts piling the leftovers onto a tray. "Let's meet back here in an hour. I've got work to finish at the office."

I follow him into the kitchen with the empty mugs.

"Thanks, Paula. Just leave them anywhere. I'll clean up later."

He's standing close enough for my heart to skip a beat.

"I don't know what our plans are, but would you like to have dinner with me tonight?" he asks right as Adam walks in and starts talking about a broken fencepost.

"… I'll need to redo the whole thing. Concrete, everything." He sees me standing in the corner and asks, "So, when do I have to give up my baby?"

"What?"

"The bass. When do you need it back?"

"I'm leaving tomorrow."

"Too bad. We'll stay up all night then, the bass and I."

"Good plan," Ben says. "Make it an unforgettable night."

I want to visit Luna and start walking toward the dog cabins, but an incoming text stops me. The real world is catching up.

First there's a voicemail from Valentina. "Big chaos here. Super serious. You need to come back. The school is sold. They're starting interviews next week. Dan says don't worry, but it's so strange. I don't know what's going on. Call me."

When Valentina is stressed, which doesn't happen often, her English sounds more Portuguese. I replay her message twice.

Then Max. "Change of plan, looking into cheap flights now. Gabriel and I are coming to Vegas."

And lastly, my ex-fiancé calling, slightly drunk. "Good, you didn't change your number. It's me, Julian. Maybe you can give me a call. Or no, don't call. I'll call you. Tomorrow. Gotta go."

Then a second one from him. "Paula? It's me again." There's a pause, then he goes on quietly. "What I want to tell you is, I can't stop thinking about you. Since the party, you know? You are so, hmm, different now. And also not, if that makes any sense."

I squeeze the phone tighter to my ear. He sounds as if he's falling asleep. "Do you think you could forgive me? I want our life back, Paulie. Remember, our life? How we used to read each other's mind, stay in bed on Sundays, and the couch we picked out together, and all our plans? I don't need to live overseas. I want to go night-skiing for five bucks again. You can get a cat if you still want one. I'm a total idiot. Miss you, baby."

I stare at the screen of my Galaxy S10. It has wrecked everything in a minute. Carefree Paula is gone. I look down at my new clothes, but they don't bring her back. She got lost inside an overpriced prism-white Korean cell phone. I throw it on the ground. Of course, it's shatterproof.

At least Julian's message should make me feel good. The man I wanted 'til death do us part, wants me back. Wasn't it only yesterday that I told Rita he's the only one for me? But then there's Ben, and every time I look at him, my brain goes offline.

Julian at the party. I was so glad to see him. Couples go through stuff, maybe the split-up was our stuff. And we've both grown, which is a good thing. All I need to do is drive home, secure the job, and work things out with him.

I pick up the phone and start walking. Why did he whisper on the phone, was his girlfriend in the other room? I walk faster. The buildings all look the same, I didn't pay attention last night. So many abandoned animals. The things people do make me sick.

I locate Luna's room from her name written on the chalkboard. I open the door and find her lying on a pile of blankets with her puppies tucked underneath her paws. Maybe it's my imagination, but she looks like she's smiling. I don't even know if animals can smile or if it's just something we'd like to believe.

She gets up and staggers toward me. I bend down and wrap my arms around her soft body, asking her for forgiveness.

"My sweet dog. If only I could take you with me."

She leans against my chest and sinks down. I cannot stand the idea that some stranger will come and take her away. I want to be the one who brings her home and makes her trust the world again. I want her to feel loved and safe when her babies get taken away, one at a time. I want to run on a beach with her and curl up on the couch together.

Pharrell Williams sings through my indestructible Samsung.

"Hi Max."

"You don't sound happy, what's up?"

"Too much for international roaming."

"You can tell me everything tomorrow. We got cheap flights to Vegas, Gabriel and I. Arriving at four p.m. We can even hang out for a bit and drive home the next day, what do you think?"

"I'll need to be back Tuesday."

"We can make that, Paula. Between the three of us driving, we'll have you at your desk on time, I promise."

"What about your boys' night in Vegas?"

"Next time. It's no big deal, really."

"Thanks Max."

"You're in this mess because of me. Now I'm getting you out. Anything else?"

"I don't even know where to start."

"Tell me everything on the ride home. It's a nineteen-hour drive. Should be fun."

My eyes start burning. Nineteen hours of pretending I'm fine. Nineteen hours away from Ben. None of this will be fun.

CHAPTER Twenty

When I get back, everybody's gathered in the parking lot. "We're all looking for you," Ben says when he sees me. "Is everything okay?"

"Sorry you had to wait."

Rita puts her arm around my shoulders. "Another troubling phone call?"

"I'll tell you later. Hey, are you leaving without your special bag?"

"I want things to be right before I bring him along."

"Vamonos, let's go." Xavier rattles the car keys. Only now do I notice his outfit. Black satin shirt, half open, golden watch and heavy necklace, his hair slicked back. Extremely tight pants over pointy dress shoes.

"I'm Tony Montana. You fuck with me, you fuckin' with the best. You little cockroaches." He chews on a toothpick, then goes on in his regular voice. "Scarface. Halloween two years ago."

"Best film ever," Adam says.

"Yeah, it's good," Xavier says. "Except dumb people buy into the stereotypes of Latinos and crime, you know. Bothers me. At least today it works in our favor."

"C'mon man, you're having fun," Adam says. "Admit it for once. And you're nailing it, too."

Ben is trying to get Bear into the car with treats, kind words, firm voice. Nothing works. Eventually, the guys lift him up and into the back, where Toto welcomes him with a friendly lick. I crawl into the back row, Xavier sits left of me, and Adam to the right. Ben holds the passenger door open for Rita, waits until she's buckled in, and then gets behind the wheel.

"Why do I smell salad?" Adam turns his head and sniffs the air.

"Here." Xavier points at his head. "I was out of gel."

"What is it?"

"Olive oil. Cold pressed, extra virgin."

Ben parks half a block away from the house. We hurry to get out of the car and across the street to avoid attention from the neighbors. Rita and I are closest to the door with the guys towering behind us. I clear my throat and ring the bell. Rita looks at me, shrugs, and rings it a second time, this time longer and with more urgency. Then she unlocks the door with her key, and we all squeeze into the hallway. I didn't expect to get in this easily.

"Now what?" Ben asks. "Do you think she's out to get moving boxes?"

Rita shakes her head. "I bet she's sitting it out, as usual."

"Then she'll have to sit with us. Let's see who lasts longer." Ben hooks in the door chain. "Why don't you give us a little tour, now that we made it this far."

Rita seems hesitant. She takes one step forward, then stops. As if a trap door could open any second. "It's harder than I thought," she says. "Someone took the life out of my home."

And the fresh air, too. It smells like a locker room.

"You guys go ahead," Xavier says. "I'll stay by the door in case things get ugly."

"Is that Tony talk or you?" I ask.

"It's me. I can kiss the green card goodbye if someone calls the cops."

Rita looks worried. "I don't want to cause any trouble for you. Let's just forget about it and go home."

"We've come so far. I'm staying." I put my arm around her.

"We're taking care of you, Rita," Ben says. "Don't worry."

Adam looks up from his phone. "I have nothing else going on. Happy to be the lookout for the Mexican chicken here." He flaps his arms like wings.

"Okay," Xavier says with a heavy Pacino accent. "Me, I want what's coming to me."

"Oh well, what's coming to you, Tony?" Adam plays along.

"The world, chico, and everything with it."

They hit each other on the shoulder, macho style, and burst out laughing. Ben lets Bear off the leash and follows them to the next room. "You guys need a new movie."

The living room is a total mess. Adam's room is a minimalist masterpiece compared to this clutter. Every surface is covered in empty food wrappers and coffee cups, paper towels, gossip magazines. One cover promises, "The Truth on Melania." "Who's Lying?" asks another one. Toto sniffs his way through a box of rice cakes and stops at a puddle of brown liquid, a dimpled can of Diet Coke beside it. Bear looks bored and starts to bark at the front door.

"You can't leave yet, old boy, we're here on a mission." Ben taps gently on his back.

"Hey man, check this out," Adam yells from the end of the hallway. "You, too, green card amigo, I promise it's worth it."

I look for Rita and find her in the kitchen, opening one cupboard after the other. There's more anger than sadness in her eyes now.

"Look at this mess. Everything's gooey and covered in dust. We should have brought gloves."

I'm too distracted by the beauty of this kitchen, a fifties gem. The cupboards are turquoise with rounded edges, the floor's a black and white checkerboard. Truly vintage, from the toaster to the chairs.

"Still dieting, old Doris. Always obsessed with her looks." Rita points at the open fridge. There are a few cans of soda, fat-free milk, and a glass of pickles.

"Can I help you with anything?" I ask.

She rummages through the drawers and doesn't seem to hear me.

"How about this?" She holds up a pile of envelopes.

They all bear the same address. Mr. Harold Porter, 3216 Seneca Drive.

"Is this the guy?" I ask.

She nods. "He's the friend who sent me the letter. Looks like they're all bills, never opened. NV Energy, Valley Telecommunications, Home Depot, oh, here's one from the IRA. No wonder he's hanging low in Arizona."

She digs through every cupboard and soon the counter is covered in junk. Hotel napkins, matches, broken sunglasses, and mostly papers.

Rita's hand glides along the rounded cabinets. "At least she didn't trash everything."

The boys seem to be having a party down the hallway. Adam's laughter is the loudest.

"Why don't you see what they're up to?" Rita says. "I'll take a closer look at these in the meantime."

She holds up Harold's mail.

I find the guys in the master bedroom. The furniture is all wood, quite old-fashioned. The wallpaper with its velvet pattern matches the pillows, and the whole room looks quite elegant. Marie Antoinette could have lived here if she'd been the queen of Vegas. But then there is a huge mirror above the bed. And red bulbs in every light fixture.

"How old is the woman who lives here?" Adam asks.

"Seventy-something."

Xavier stares at the framed photographs on the wall.

"Holy smokes. Is that her?"

I move closer and nod. Even though we've only had a short encounter, I recognize the woman in the pictures. Lola alone, Lola kicking her legs with the troupe, Lola backstage with tassels. And in every picture, Lola is topless.

"Man, am I ever glad I came along. This beats the shit out of fixing fences." Adam flicks on the switch for the bedside lamp and leans toward the photos. "She's hot."

"These pics must be forty years old," Xavier says.

"I like vintage."

"Is that why you're single?"

Adam grabs a book from the bedside table and throws it at Xavier. It misses his head by an inch and cracks the mirror of the dressing table.

"And that'll be seven years of bad luck," Ben says. "Not sure if that goes for the owner of the mirror, or for the one who broke it."

"I'm not superstitious," Adam says and picks up the book. "*The Notebook*, who would have thought our girl Lola's a romantic."

"In the end we all want the same," Ben says, and I blush.

"What is this?" Rita pops her head through the door. "What did she do to our bedroom?"

"It wasn't fifty shades of red before?" Adam asks.

She shakes her head.

"It's not that bad, Rita. Once her furniture's out, we'll give it a good scrub." I slide the window open. "Just imagine the whole place empty."

She looks absent-minded as she picks up the perfume bottles on the dresser and puts them back in a neat line. She opens the top drawer. It looks like a freshly stocked bin at Walgreen's. Curlers, lipsticks, nail polish, everything's neatly organized by color, size, and purpose. How strange when the rest of the house is such a mess. Another drawer houses an assortment of wigs and hair pieces. Black ponytails, platinum curls, long, short, curly, straight, tiaras and pearls—enough props for a Broadway show. It takes both of us to push the stuff down in order to close the drawer.

"I've never been to a showgirl's bedroom," Adam says. "Why don't you try some of that stuff on?"

"I doubt you'll make it to anyone's bedroom if you say stuff like that." Ben holds one of the perfume bottles in Adam's face like bear spray. "Care for some Opium?" He looks at the label before pushing the nozzle. "Yves Saint Laurent."

The cloying Oriental scent settles over the room and makes all three guys jump up and leave. Bear trots behind them, while Toto sticks to Rita like Velcro.

"This one's definitely expired," Rita says and fans her face with one hand. "Look at this mess now."

She opens the walk-in closet. Or rather, attempts to, since the door is blocked by a heap of crumpled garments. It looks as if the wardrobe has been attacked by troops and left to die. A battlefield of sequins and dust bunnies. With everything piled on the floor, the built-in racks have nothing to hold. One lace bustier hibernates on a lonely hanger. A feather boa entangled with fishnet stockings is lurking on the top shelf. This graveyard of costumes hasn't been aired in years and the dust makes me cough. I head for the hallway. Nothing in this house makes sense. It's like trying to build a puzzle whose pieces come from three different sets.

"What does this woman live on?" Adam calls from the kitchen. "There's nothing in the fridge. I might have to do a pizza run."

"You can't be hungry again," Ben says. He leans against the windowsill with his arms crossed. "The dogs don't even beg for food, and you had a ton for breakfast."

"Keeping track now, are we?" Adam comes back to the living room. "I get in a bad mood when I'm hungry. Just trying to make it easier for you guys." He throws his bony body on the loveseat.

Xavier looks up from *Us Weekly*. "Copia ciborum, subtilitas impeditur. Seneca."

"Huh?" Adam looks at him.

"The abundance of food hampers intelligence."

"The fuck's that supposed to mean?"

"The address, Seneca Drive, and all you want to do is stuff yourself. Just saying."

"Not all of us went to posh private schools, you know. With your Latin quotes and housekeepers, and father in the government."

"Guys, come on, what's all the bickering about? Xavier just made a little joke, okay?" Ben puts his hand on Adam's shoulder.

"It's okay, I'm not offended," Xavier says. "What you don't seem to understand, Adam, is that my sheltered little life didn't get me very far, did it? My father threw me out of the house, and you walked away from yours. And here we are, all in the same place, trying to build a new life and pay the bills."

He goes back to his magazine and flips the pages without reading. Adam stares at the floor like an angry toddler.

"On second thought," Ben says, "maybe you could go for a takeout and get Rita a new lock at the same time. There's a hardware store in the strip mall on Desert Inn Road."

"Hmm." Adam is sulking in his loveseat.

"Take this for the lock."

He gives him his credit card and the car keys. Then he sits next to me on the couch.

"I don't know what that was all about, we usually get along fine. Maybe it's the house. Bad vibes or something."

He's right, there's a heaviness in the air.

"My sister does this thing she calls 'cleansing the energy' before she moves into a new place. I'm sure she'll help Rita turn this into a happy house again."

Xavier smiles. "Remember the incense we had to burn in every room? Honestly, it's a good thing I'd known you for a while, because Ava seemed pretty crazy to me."

"You don't have to tell me."

"But good crazy, you know. I just love her."

They'd make a perfect couple, Ava and Xavier.

"I'll marry her in my next life," he says.

"Did your father really throw you out?" I regret asking the second I hear myself.

"Yes, my father cut me out of his life. I haven't seen him in ten years."

"I'm sorry."

"You get used to it."

Xavier keeps his eyes down. "It's strange because I used to be close to my father as a kid. The only boy among three girls, you know. He'd take me to soccer games and baseball, always hoping I'd turn into a jock. But it wasn't really my thing, and as I got older, almost every conversation turned into a fight."

"I know the feeling, happened with me and my mom."

He smiles at me. "It got worse. On my twentieth birthday I told my parents that I was in love, and that his name was Eduardo. Actually, Eduardo was right there in the living room with us when I told them. My old man left the house without a word, and when he came back, he asked me to leave and not come back until I was, 'normal' again."

"Have you been back to Mexico?"

"I went to my sister's wedding. We all promised not to spoil her day and sort of managed. But I've never set foot in our family home again."

"And your mother?"

"Once a year she visits her cousin, in Arizona." Xavier inserts the last two words in air quotes. "Which is true in that she flies to Phoenix and spends one night there. The rest of the time she stays with us."

"Bingo." Rita shouts from the bedroom. "I found something." She runs down the hallway with a shoebox in her hand. Toto barks with excitement.

"This here could be enough to get my house back."

"What's in there, ruby slippers?" Xavier asks.

Rita smiles. "That would have worked, too. But no, look at this."

She shows us the contents of the box. A bottle of Wite-Out, scissors, glue, and a pile of official-looking envelopes. Then she hands me one of the letters. It's a doctor's note.

"Mr. Harold Porter of 3216 Seneca Dr., born July 29th, 1937, suffers from constructive pulmonary heart disease and is dependent on home oxygen therapy. Reliable access to electricity is therefore essential for the patient."

It ends with a stamp and an illegible scrawl. I pass the piece of paper to Ben, not sure what Harold's heart has to do with Rita's house.

"There are four more in here." She sounds excited.

"They're from four different walk-in clinics, and they all attest that home oxygen therapy is vital for the resident of this address."

She holds the piece of paper up against the light. "If you look carefully, you can see that the color is slightly off right here. Lola has been forging the dates ever since Harold moved out."

I still don't know why this is such a big deal.

"She's not paying the electricity bills, so at some point she'd sit in the dark. But if you can prove that one of the residents has a medical condition requiring constant access to electricity, they can't turn off the power."

"How do you know all that?" Ben asks.

"Temping at a law office," she says and taps the side of her forehead. "At least it was good for something."

"How long can she get away with this?" He puts the note back in the envelope.

"As long as she doesn't get caught, I guess. Or until she finds the next guy who's willing to pay for everything."

"But shouldn't all that be in your name?" I ask. "You're the owner after all."

"I have no idea how they were able to put it into Harold's."

Rita pulls two more letters out of the box. They're addressed to Frank and Rita Valione, and they've both been opened.

"Payment reminders from when Harold first moved in," she says. "One's for electricity, and the other one's for the phone. Technically speaking, that's mail theft."

She beams with excitement.

"Ben, honey, the phone's right behind you. Would you try it for me, please?"

He picks it up. "Dead."

"That's what I thought," Rita sings and stuffs everything back in the box.

"As soon as Adam comes back with the lock, we'll empty the place," Ben says. "It shouldn't take more than an hour to throw it all out."

"Are you sure you want to go through with this?" Rita asks.

"Don't worry, I can handle a crazy showgirl."

"Me, too," Xavier agrees. "And if the cops get involved, I'll just jump over the neighbor's wall. That's our thing, apparently. Jumping walls, dealing drugs."

"And the big hats, don't forget those," Ben says.

"Of course, that's who we are. Sombrero wearing, wall-climbing hombres on drugs."

"Viva el stereotype," Ben says and bangs his fist on the coffee table. This upsets Toto who now starts running in circles, yapping incessantly, and nibbling Bear's hind leg. Rita tries to pick him up, but he's fast and slides out of her hand each time.

"Come on, little guy, it's all good," Ben says with a soothing voice, but the dog doesn't want to settle.

"He can run it off outside," Rita says and fumbles with the strings of the patio blinds.

When she steps outside the smile dies on her lips. We follow her outside.

"What has she done to my backyard?"

A single camping chair stands lost amidst the carpet of cigarette butts. The lifeless stump with the burn marks must have been a palm tree at one time. Ben hits an empty Coleman cooler with his foot and a hundred ants start running for their lives.

"Nooo," Rita screams as her eyes follow the ant trail onto the dried-up lawn.

What used to be a swimming pool is filled with plastic bags and garbage in various stages of decay. The kidney-shaped field of trash is spilling across the lawn, and a nauseating stench fills the air. Milk cartons, rotten fruit and leftovers have morphed into a pelt of mold. Empty bottles stick out like gun barrels, and the skeleton of a Christmas tree still bears a string of red tinsel while it's drowning in waste.

We stand around like a family at an open grave. Bear is sniffing the air, nostrils wide open. Toto, irritated by Rita's scream, runs toward the pool like a cartoon dog, his tiny legs in overdrive. He fails to stop and dives right into the dump. Looking somewhat confused, he tries to walk on the wobbly surface, while Rita yells his name. He sinks deep into one spot, digs himself back up to the surface, then waddles off in the opposite direction.

"Toto, come back this way."

He appears to move toward her, when suddenly something brownish runs across a Safeway bag and vanishes from sight. The dog shoots around and starts chasing the furry thing to the bottom of the pool. His shrill barking sounds muffled as he digs himself into the deep end.

"Toto," Rita shouts in a panic. "He's going to suffocate."

"I'll get him." Ben jumps into the stinking garbage pit.

The dog looks surprised at the sight of a six-foot human worming his way toward him, and he interrupts the rodent chase just long enough for Ben to grab him by the collar.

"Here you are," he says and hands him to Rita. Toto shakes his body, then stands still as Rita puts him on the leash. Bear, who's watched the whole scene from the distance, is coming closer and starts licking the little dog.

"What did I miss?" Adam appears out of nowhere.

"How did you get in here?" Xavier asks.

"Nobody heard me at the door, so I climbed the gate over there. Seriously man, what are you doing?"

Adam stays a few feet away from Ben and flicks something spaghetti-like from his shirt. "You need a shower."

"Fresh clothes, too, if you want to ride in the car with us," Xavier says as they walk across the lawn. Rita and I follow behind. The sad look on her face has turned to anger.

"Lola definitely crossed the line," she says. "I felt sorry for her when I saw her things in the bedroom. She's spent her whole life trying to look young and find love in the wrong places, and yet she always ended up alone. But that doesn't give her the right to destroy what's dear to me. Let's get to work."

CHAPTER Twenty-one

We head back toward the bathroom as Toto needs to be washed. Ben's clothes are piled on the floor, and I hear Adam's voice coming from the walk-in closet.

"Everything's a size four. Not your lucky day, man."

Ben opens the door, wearing nothing but boxer shorts and the body of a Greek god. "We'll skip the shower. Someone hasn't paid the water bill either."

"What do you mean?" Xavier asks.

We all squeeze inside the bathroom.

"See?" Ben points at a portable camping toilet. An eight-gallon water dispenser sits on the sink along with several boxes of wet wipes. He smells one and makes a face.

"Now with more aloe," he reads from the box and starts rubbing his chest.

Adam comes back with a short burgundy robe. "Here, try this. The only thing that'll fit you."

Ben puts it on and turns toward me.

"What do you think?" he says. "Is this someone you'd have dinner with?"

The stitching on one breast pocket says *Playboy Club*, with a smaller *Des Moines, Iowa* on the other.

"I would," Adam says before me.

Idiot. He ruined the moment again.

Rita has dragged a pile of flattened cardboard across the floor and starts making boxes.

"Let me help you." I take one of the boxes.

"They were still in the old spot in the garage. I always thought I'd be using them with Frank."

The last time I packed moving boxes was when Julian left. They were supposed to go into storage while we were in Australia.

"I almost forgot," Adam says. "A brand-new lock for you, Rita, and some treats for everyone."

He puts a take-out tray in front of us. "Don't tell Ava," he says. "Supporting McDonald's is right up there with killing puppies."

"Why did you go then?" Ben asks, slightly annoyed.

"Had to use their washroom. Won't happen again."

"She's got a lot of things for a squatter." Rita throws everything from the shelves into a box and stuffs a pillow on top. Then she pounds on the load with the brass base of the table lamp. She keeps hitting it until we hear something break inside the box.

"It's liberating, you should try it," Rita says and holds the lamp up for grabs.

"May I?" Adam asks. "Apparently I have anger issues from my childhood." He takes a good hit at one of the boxes and smiles. "Finally, a therapy that's efficient and fun."

Rita picks up two porcelain figurines, a lady in a ruffled dress, and a boy playing the violin.

"You go first," Adam says.

Rita takes the lamp back from him and looks at the figurines from all sides.

"We won't trash them," she says. "Somebody made them, with their hands." She wraps them in paper and puts them in a box. "They look happy."

"What about Goodwill?" Ben suggests. "Lola can buy it all back if she wants."

Rita likes the idea and Ben makes a few calls from his cell phone.

"One of their vans is in the neighborhood right now. They'll try to get ahold of the driver and send him here."

We get back to work and have six boxes filled quickly. A knock on the front door stops us dead in our tracks.

"It can't be Lola, she's got her key," Rita says and gets up.

I'm relieved to see a gray-haired gentleman with a cane. His eyes are kind, but his mouth is ready to express anger. Before he says anything, he studies each one of us and his chin relaxes. Bear lets out a throaty bark.

"Can I help you with anything?" Rita asks.

"I'd like to talk to the person who lives here."

"That would be me, as of now."

"Pleased to meet you, my name's Richard." He extends his hand.

"Hi Richard, I'm Rita."

"I'm your next-door neighbor and I heard all the commotion outside. Is everything fine?"

"I apologize for the noise, it's all settled now."

"It's just that, I complained about the smell to the previous tenant a number of times, but nothing ever changed. I thought she's added dogs to the mess now, and well, you can imagine. But I am delighted to see that I was wrong."

"We're working on cleaning up the mess," Rita says. "I do have a dog, though."

"I look forward to meeting him. Let me know if you need anything. I'm home most days." He pulls a card from his wallet and gives it to Rita.

"Actually, Richard, we could use your help," Ben says, hiding the Playboy stitching with one hand. "Would you have some tools we can borrow? We need to put in a new lock."

"It would be my pleasure," Richard says. "And once the kids have moved you in, allow me to extend an invitation for a welcome drink, Rita."

"That would be lovely."

She watches him walk away until he's out of sight.

"I guess we won't have to worry about Rita being lonely," Adam says. "That's one classy dude."

"He is quite handsome, isn't he?" Rita says and reads the full name of his card "Richard Cooper, MD, Ophthalmologist."

Adam looks over her shoulder. "If you can read that without glasses, you won't need an eye doctor."

"The next person at the door might be Lola," Ben says. "How should we handle this, good cop—bad cop, or do you want to sit her down for a talk?"

"I'm out of patience," Rita says. "And I don't want her to set foot in my house again."

"Look what the woman did to our sweet Rita here." Adam puts his arm around her. "I'd say, good cop's not home today. She's going to deal with Tony Montana and the dogs."

We all agree.

"And you, Paula," Adam continues. "I know you're Canadian and all, but you've got to keep your 'sorry' and 'excuse me' down. You'll need to toughen up."

"I like her just the way she is." Ben looks at me from the side.

Adam's know-it-all attitude has annoyed me all day.

"She'd lose to that stripper, just saying."

"Don't patronize me, Adam. You bet your hippie ass, I can stand up for myself."

I feel both relieved and embarrassed and I want to say sorry, but I wash the impulse down with the rest of my McCoffee.

Adam cracks a smile. "I think this is the beginning of a beautiful friendship," he says.

"That's not *Scarface*."

"*Casablanca* is second best."

CHAPTER Twenty-two

It's close to five and the house is almost empty. We watch the Goodwill truck leave with the first load of boxes and furniture.

"And you're sure you don't want to keep any of that?" Ben asks Rita as they start taking the bed apart.

"I'd rather not sleep at all."

"We have an empty guest room at Noah's right now. You're welcome to stay until you're ready to move in."

"Thanks, I may take you up on that." Rita squeezes Ben's arm.

She turns the last drawer of the vanity upside down and dumps its contents into a box. A perfume bottle slips away and hits the ground. I mop up the sticky mix of orchid and musk with a blond wig.

"How can I ever thank you for what you've done?" Rita says. "Meeting you has changed my life."

"I feel the same," Ben says. He's standing close to me and nobody else heard him.

"When are you leaving, Paula?" Xavier asks from underneath the bed.

"My friend's flying in tomorrow afternoon, and we'll be leaving right away."

"Woah, what's the hurry?" Adam says and pulls out his phone. "According to Google Maps, you'll make Vegas to Vancouver in nineteen hours and fifty-three minutes. No reason to stress. You can stay here till Tuesday morning if you have a couple of drivers."

Yes, if I want to look like a zombie at the interview.

"Say something, I just gave you a bonus day."

"Thanks. And sorry for what I said earlier."

"Forget it, we're even. I may have pushed your buttons a bit." He clears his throat. "I am sorry, too."

Xavier resurfaces and dusts off his pants. "This thing won't come apart. We might need a saw. Let's see if the vanity is any lighter."

The smooth wood, now uncluttered and bare, is quite nice. I picture a Hollywood beauty brushing her hair while her beau leans in the doorway with a martini.

"I like this dresser," Ben says. "So fifties."

As if he read my mind again, I let my fingers glide along the curved wood.

"Would you mind stepping aside for a second?" Xavier taps on my shoulder.

"Of course." I move over and make space for the guys. They push and pull and curse before they manage to move it three inches from the wall.

"Dios mio, look at this mess." Xavier points at the things that have collected behind the dresser over the years. Paper tissues, rollers, and hairballs everywhere. Underneath all that I see a brown paper bag. It looks like forgotten trash, but when I pick it up, I see that it's neatly folded and held together with an elastic band. I shake off the dust and call Rita.

"You might want to check it out, maybe more forged letters."

She opens the bag and looks inside.

"What is it?" Adam asks.

Rita shakes her head in disbelief and holds the bag open for us to see. It's full of dollar bills.

"Who's still getting paid in cash?" Adam says.

Ben points at the mirror above the bed.

"No way. You think this is her, um, office?"

Ben starts to count the bills.

"Two thousand eight hundred and fifty dollars," he says. "That'll take care of the pool cleanup."

Rita looks at the money as if it's a dead rat. "I don't want any of it."

"But Rita, you'll have expenses before you can move in," Ben says. "A few things need to be fixed. I think you should keep it."

She looks absent-minded and keeps shaking her head.

"All I want is to just get my house back. If it wasn't for all of you, I wouldn't even be here. Please, take it for the animals."

"That's generous of you, Rita, but really, it's yours. Consider it rental income. Do you have any idea how much this house would have made you each month?"

"And that doesn't include the business license," Adam says.

She thinks for a moment, then takes half of the bills and gives the rest to Ben.

"For Noah's Bark," she says. "Maybe that'll help get the new project started that Ava mentioned."

"Thank you, you're very sweet." Ben slides the money into the chest pocket of his robe.

"Great, now your sister will start talking about the pig rescue again. Just so you know—I'll veto it." Adam moans. "And you look like a pimp."

"There won't be a vote. She's doing it."

CHAPTER Twenty-three

At first, I don't even hear that someone's fumbling with the front door. Even though Richard had come back with a screwdriver right away, the discovery of the money got in the way of changing the lock.

Clack, crick, the door opens as far as the chain allows, then bounces back and slams shut right away. I lean out of the bedroom to get a glimpse of the door. Bear is sleeping in the living room, his paws twitching. The last time I saw Toto, he was in the kitchen licking crumbs from under the table. Great watch dogs.

I squeeze Rita's arm and point at the entrance. There's more fiddling with the chain, this time the door remains open one crack, just enough for a bony hand to fit through and feel up and down the edge of the door, trying to gain access.

"Showtime," Ben says as we sneak along the hallway toward the door. I smell cigarette smoke as we get closer. Rita takes a step forward and speaks through the gap without releasing the chain.

"You're late, Lola," she says. "Didn't we say twelve noon?"

"Shut up and open the door." Lola takes a puff from her cigarette and stretches her scrawny neck to get a look past Rita. "What's going on in there? Open up." She bangs against the door.

"It's over, Lola. You don't live here anymore." Rita unhooks the chain and opens the door wider.

"Get out of the way." Lola tries to shove her aside.

The noise catches Toto's attention. He flies out of the kitchen and jumps into Rita's arms, baring his teeth at Lola. That in turn wakes up Bear. He trots toward the door and squeezes his head between the two women. Lola stumbles as she tries to get away from the slobbering dog. She takes a deep breath and looks furious.

"What the hell do you want?"

"Isn't that obvious?" Rita says. "I want you out of my life."

"Bah," Lola coughs. "That'll take more than a couple of mutts. I know guys who can take them out like that." She snaps her fingers in Rita's face. "Who are these clowns and what's he doing in my robe?"

"It's just until my clothes have dried," Ben says. "I went for a swim in your pool."

"Is he on drugs?" Lola asks, then she looks at me.

"We met last night, don't you remember?" I ask. "And these are my assistants."

She laughs in my face. "Oh yeah? Where did you find them, at the Halloween store?" She sucks the last bit of her cigarette and drops the butt.

"Littering, how I hate that," Ben says and points at the ground. "Especially when it's not even your house."

"I don't have to listen to this. I live here. Now get out of my way and take those damn dogs with you."

She points at Bear, the keyring still in her hand. He takes it as an invitation to play and licks her hand with his thick, wet tongue. Lola shrieks and drops the keys. Before she has a chance to react, Xavier grabs them and slides them into his pocket.

"Now listen carefully, baby doll," he says, cracking his knuckles and taking a big step toward her. "You don't live here anymore. This is our house, nuestra casa. Comprende?"

"What's he talking about?" she asks me.

"You see, Ms. Frimp, isn't it? We were trying to be nice yesterday, give you some time to prepare. Unfortunately, you didn't use it wisely, so we may have rushed it a little."

I open the door all the way and show her the empty house.

"What the hell did you do?"

"We want to make sure your belongings are in a safe place and we feel that the Goodwill store is best suited. What's the street again, Ben?"

"Nellis Boulevard," he says.

"Right, the Goodwill on Nellis Boulevard will safeguard your things until you're ready to take them off their hands again, no rush."

"You didn't." Lola's face turns the same color as her nails. Somewhere in the distance a police car turns on the horn and Bear starts howling.

"Damn you, Harold," she mumbles to herself. "I told him to change that stupid lock."

For a moment she looks as if she's ready to give up. But then she opens her purse and decides otherwise. To my relief she doesn't pull out a gun, just her cell phone.

"And whom would you like to call?" Ben asks and tightens the belt of his robe.

"Not that it's any of your fucking business, but I'm calling the cops. They can ask the neighbors. I live here."

"So, you know this gentleman then?" Ben points at Richard in his driveway. He waves at Rita before he gets into his white Cadillac.

"Of course, I do. It's what's-his-name, the uptight guy next door."

She starts to punch something into her phone, but Adam rips it from her hand before she finishes. He turns the phone off and throws it back at her.

"I wouldn't get the cops involved, if I were you, lady. I'm not sure if you go to prison for forging doctors' notes and shit, but you'll sure as hell work for a long time to pay off those bills. We found everything."

Her lips are trembling. "I know people in Vegas. You'll see. You'll all see."

"Careful with your threats," Ben says calmly. "Please understand that we have copies of everything that went on in this house. Mail fraud is a serious matter."

Lola stands in the middle of the walkway, motionless, deflated.

"Take this and find your peace." Rita puts a small bundle in her hand. "It's a shame that someone with your looks and talent had to go so low."

She turns and disappears into the house.

"I hate you," Lola screams. "I hate you all. What the hell are you doing with these freaks here, you boring old cow? I never understood what Frank saw in you."

"You'd better stop right there before I forget my good manners," Ben says. "Now get in your car, and don't say another word."

"And how do you want me to open the car? That guy took my keys." She points at Xavier. "Freaking fruit picker."

"Unbelievable." Ben shakes his head.

"Give me the keys."

"You're in no position to make demands, and there are only two options. Apologize or walk." Ben stares at her without blinking.

She looks down, chewing the inside of her cheek.

"Come on guys, let's not waste our time," Ben says. "Someone's going for a walk today."

"The keys." Her voice is trembling. "Please give me the keys."

Xavier takes the house key off the chain.

"Wait," Ben says. "That wasn't much of an apology."

"What do you want me to say?"

"Have you never said, 'I'm sorry' in your life?"

She looks at Xavier for one second.

"Sorry if I offended you or something."

He gives her the key. "You could never offend me."

Ben takes her by the arm and walks her to the car, Bear by his side.

"If you ever show up in this neighborhood, he will chew you up. Like a turkey neck."

She lowers the window and looks at Ben.

"Screw you. Screw you all."

"You wish," Adam yells as she speeds off.

Rita sits at the table, lost in thought.

"You did it, she's out of your life." I put my arms around her. She's trembling.

"What was in that pouch you gave her?"

"The two figurines and the family portrait." She wipes her eyes and leans into me.

"You're a saint, Rita."

We stay like this for a while, and I watch Ben put in the new lock. He's up right next to her on the scale of goodness. Or rather, no. He's too hot for a saint.

CHAPTER Twenty-four

"**I'm hungry," Adam** says about five minutes into the car ride.

"Again?" Xavier and Ben ask simultaneously.

"That was a lot of work in there."

"Are you a diabetic?" I ask Adam.

"Who knows? I'm not a doctor."

"Oh, come on, you have nothing," Ben says. "You're just really cranky between meals. Do you seriously expect me to go to a restaurant dressed like this?" He points at his bare legs.

Xavier suggests a taqueria that's on our way. "It's soccer night, nobody cares what you look like."

When we get to Don Felipe Del Desierto, Xavier is greeted with hugs and kisses by the owners. After he introduces us, we're all treated like family and get the best table in the house, right by the TV set where Mexico is playing Uruguay. It's impossible to understand a word anyone says, as the wall-mounted speakers for the stereo are blaring Spanish power ballads throughout the restaurant, and the volume of the TV is being turned up every time there's a goal, or almost goal, or a should-have-been-a-goal.

Rita and I just have a side order of guacamole and nachos. During the half-time break, the owners join us at the table. They're a kind couple in their sixties, and Xavier tells us that he helped them build an addition to their house. There's a lot of hugging and laughing going on, and I wish I could remember some of the Spanish I took in grade twelve.

"*Esto es mi amigo Ben*," Xavier says and puts one arm around him.

"*Vaya Ben*," Xavier says. "*Pratique el espanol*, practice, my friend. You'll need it soon."

"I'm not ready for conversation."

"Come on, you know how my English sounded when we first met. Just have to go for it."

"Okay, here it goes." Ben clears his throat. "*Mi zapatero es rico*."

Don Felipe and his wife look at each other, then simultaneously ask, "Que?"

"*Mi zapatero es rico*," Ben repeats even more slowly.

"Why would you tell them that your shoemaker is rich?" Xavier asks.

"Chapter four: Out and About."

"I didn't know you were planning a trip to the fifties."

Ben's practice time is up, as Mexico and Uruguay are back in position. With his country being in the lead, Don Felipe supports his team by cranking up the volume to the max. I have no idea how Xavier manages to answer his phone and, from the look of it, understand everything the person on the other end says. Uruguay scores, two Mexicans cry, Adam spills his beer, and the owner's wife brings us Tequila.

An equalizing goal and a dozen hugs later, we're back in the car. I feel as if I've just been across the border and back, all in forty-five minutes.

"Do you mind dropping me off at the bar?" Xavier asks. "Marco just called. One waiter's sick and the bartender cut his hand on a broken glass."

He takes off his gold watch and jewelry. "Not much I can do about my greasy hair." He looks at his reflection in the window. "Marco is my partner," he says to Rita and me. "He's got a cocktail bar downtown. Sunday's karaoke night. Why don't you all come?"

"Raincheck," Ben says. "The only place I'm dressed for is the Playboy Mansion." He stops at a busy intersection and Xavier jumps out of the car.

"You're right. See you tomorrow, guys. And Paula, you'll need to come back if you want to sing at the world's best karaoke bar."

When we get back, Adam takes Rita to the dog wash station. Toto still smells like rotten fish after his adventure in the pool.

Ben and I are alone in the parking lot. Bear's waiting next to Ben and looks at me with his sagging eyes. I pet his head.

"He always looks sad."

"It's genetic. St. Bernard dogs are prone to droopy eyes. But look at his wagging tail. He's actually happy."

I look at Bear as if his rhythmic panting is the most fascinating thing in the world.

"Would you like to join me for a walk?" Ben asks. "We always check on the animals at the end of the day."

"Uh-huh, sure, that would be nice."

"I need a shower, it won't take long. Meet me at the house in ten?"

My voice has failed me again. All I can do is nod and smile like an idiot. An idiot with a flushed face who can't recall the day of the week. Or how many miles there are between here and home.

CHAPTER Twenty-five

I change into a clean shirt and look in the mirror. Before I get to brush my teeth, Valentina calls.

"Paula, I've been trying to get ahold of you for days. Did you get my texts? Where are you and what are you doing?"

"I'm in a motorhome in Las Vegas, long story."

"Have you heard the news? Has Dan talked to you yet? I'm so upset."

"That's why I'll drive back tomorrow. But I'll be home in time, guaranteed." I line my lips and dab on some gloss. "Would you say an invitation for a walk is like a date?"

"So, you know about the school." She sounds relieved. "Wait, did you say you have a date?"

"I don't know, more like an evening walk."

"Listen amiga, with the right attitude anything can a date. It's up to you. But what do you want me to do about the other thing?"

"What other thing?"

"The last text I sent you. Your ex, Julian."

"What about him?"

My lips are too sticky. I look for a tissue.

"He showed up at our place this morning, looking pretty rough. He wants to know where you are."

"What?" I sit down. "How do you guys even know him?"

"He works at Philip's office, that's why he was invited to the party. But honestly, I had no idea he was the same person that you always called, the-idiot-I-lived-with, until he dropped by today."

"What did he want?"

"I didn't get the whole story. We were about to leave the house, but he wants me to tell you that he's waiting for you. And that he regrets everything."

"Shit."

"Tell me about your date."

"Not much to tell. Great guy, lives in Vegas. The end."

"At least you're being adventurous. Oh, I forgot, Julian brought roses for you."

I sink deeper into the couch.

"Paula, are you still there?"

"What color?"

"Yellow, with soft pink edges. They're gorgeous."

For two years I've been waiting for a sign from him. Something that says he still thinks of me. That he's sorry for what happened.

And now roses.

We'd been together for a couple of months and had our first fight. There was a lot of yelling and Julian left. The next morning, he came back with twenty-one roses. He said they're called Peace Rose, and that, should he ever again fail to find the right words, I should remember these petals and how the colors complement each other. "Just like us, Paula."

They must have been hard to find in November.

"The man is determined. He's even looking at houses, he told Philip."

"What do you mean?"

"He wants to make an offer on a house. Apparently, it's an easy commute and it has a cat door. He thinks it's a sign."

"I don't understand. He's engaged to be married."

"Are you sitting? The wedding's off."

We hang up. Why is all this happening now? When I locked my apartment on Monday, I had a job, a plan, and an ex-fiancé who belonged in the past.

And here I am, at a dog shelter, fantasizing about someone I just met, and the guy who broke my heart wants to have a cat with me. If life were a game of Scrabble, I was just about to score with SCHEDULE. But then someone tripped over the board and the letters say ULSDEHEC. Which means nothing, not even in an Ikea catalogue.

Just as I'm about to knock, Ben opens the door, his hair still wet. He puts on a sweater and I realize I forgot to bring mine. We walk side by side. The stillness of the desert reminds me of winter nights in the mountains when the snow muffles every sound.

"I was afraid you might have changed your mind," he says.

"Sorry I kept you waiting."

The sky looks as though someone has thrown a bucket of lights in the air. Julian knew all about the star constellations and what they're called. I think it bothered him that I didn't remember anything the next time.

"I wish I were one of those guys who could point at the stars and talk about the Bears and the Dippers. I like that part in movies." Ben looks skyward. "But I simply can't see it."

"Me neither."

"How about the Northern star?"

"Nothing."

"Do you think it's a medical condition, like dyslexia for stars?"

"It's called dys-astronicism. I've got it, too."

"So, you're saying my past diagnosis of unromantic was wrong?" he asks.

"You can sue for malpractice."

"You're right, I should."

He slides his hand into mine and we keep walking until we reach the end of the pathway. It feels so natural, inevitable almost, and at the same time my heart is hammering in my chest, sending jolts of electricity through my body. Then he turns to face me. I want to touch him, feel his skin, but something's holding me back. Like pressing the gas and brakes at the same time. The things Valentina said about Julian are still in my head.

Ben kisses the inside of my hand, slowly, one kiss at a time. I close my eyes and hope he won't stop. When he reaches the inside of my elbow, all thought of Julian is gone. I touch Ben's hair, stroke the back of his head.

He lets go of my hand and wraps his arms around my body while his lips caress my face. His skin is soft against mine, he must be freshly shaved. And then we kiss. It feels as if it were the first kiss of my life. Or the last. As if we recognized each other after a lifetime apart. There are only his lips, our lips. I don't know what's mine or his anymore. I open my eyes.

"I wanted to do this all day," he says.

"Why didn't you?"

He puts his hand around my face and kisses me again. "The idea of it was just as delicious."

He takes off his sweater and puts it around me. "You're shivering, let's go inside."

The checkup round must be the fastest in the history of Noah's Bark. We run from one building to the next and Ben opens each door with the speed of a firefighter. He turns on the light, makes sure the number of dogs matches the names on the chalkboard and tops up water bowls where needed. We hold hands on our way back to the house and only stop once to kiss.

The lights are off, only the low humming sound of the fridge tells me that we're coming in through the kitchen. Without letting go of my hand, Ben opens a cupboard door. The clinking of glasses lingers while he leads me to the next room. There's a glow from the fireplace and I recognize the living room. It feels much bigger now with just the two of us.

He goes to put a fresh log on the embers and I already miss his touch. When he turns back to face me, my legs are Jell-O. He gently twists a strand of my hair around his finger and lets it glide down.

"Where have you been?" He pulls me closer. "I've been waiting for you all of my life."

I don't know how long we've been lying on the couch together, an hour, a minute, it all feels the same.

"There are more rooms in this house, you know." His hands rest on the small of my back.

"We haven't even had a proper first date." I move closer until I feel his heartbeat.

"The nachos didn't count?"

I shake my head.

"You've seen me without a shirt already."

"That was a teaser, not a date."

He sits up and takes my hand.

"Then I'll invite you to a midnight dinner, just you and me."

He leads me to the kitchen, pulls out a bar stool and hands me a glass of wine. I take one sip, afraid to lose the taste of his kiss. He opens the fridge and piles half of its content on the counter.

"Mushrooms, carrots, tofu, rice. Anything here that you don't like?"

"It all looks great." I would eat cobwebs with him.

He rinses the mushrooms and puts the frying pan on the stove.

"Can I help with anything?"

"You're on vacation, all-in." We kiss until I smell burnt oil.

I feel as if I've borrowed someone else's life. Never before has a first date ended anywhere further than an embrace. Not even with Julian. And I was crazy for him when we first met, that freezing day on the ski hill. We talked for hours at the lodge after I had fallen from the T-bar lift and lost one ski. To make me feel better, he went down in the gondola with me instead of racing through the powder with his friends.

But this is completely different. Ben doesn't feel like a stranger to me. There's something so familiar about his whole being that it's only natural I'm here with him, in this house, watching him cook.

"Where's Bear?" I ask.

"Probably sleeping off the excitement of the day. He usually spends his days dozing in the shade."

Ben stirs the rice.

"What do you do when you're not picking up girls and dogs from the shelter?"

"Let's see," he says, one finger on his lip. "I'm afraid that's pretty much all I do, looking for dogs and Canadians."

He scoops the tofu and garlic out of the marinade and adds it to the sizzling oil. Then he empties a bag of trail mix on the counter and combs through it with his fingers. "I only need the peanuts."

He lines them up on a cutting board and crushes them with the blade of a chef's knife.

"Isn't there a fairy tale where the girl must separate beans from sand?" he asks.

"Lentils from ashes. Cinderella."

"Does the prince cook them for her?"

"No, but that would be a better ending."

He lights a candle and puts it between our plates. Then he takes my hand and leads me to the table.

"I would have picked you up at home, but you're already here."

I just fell in love.

"So, what does an ordinary day in your life really look like?"

"I'm a high school teacher, social studies and English. But I got laid off last summer, so my days look pretty much like this one." He takes a sip of wine. "A lot of programs got canceled, and I had low seniority at my school."

"Is it that bad in all of Vegas?"

"All of Nevada."

"Would you consider working someplace else?"

"Yes, actually, I'll be moving soon."

Hopefully closer to Canada.

"I've just been hired by a private school. In Santiago."

I hope there's a Santiago in Idaho. Or North Dakota. Like Athens, Georgia.

"Santiago, Chile?"

"Yes, the school year starts in March."

"That—that's far."

I empty the whole glass so I won't have to look at him.

"I thought it would be an interesting change. It's only a two-year contract. Just enough to pay the bills until my book is out. And a paid return flight for Christmas."

"Your book?"

Maybe there's a chance he gets published fast and that the book becomes a bestseller and he won't have to leave.

"I'm a photographer, and for me there's no better place than Nevada, but sometimes you have to take a little detour."

No. A word starting with "de" is never good. Detest, decease, destroy.

"Have you ever been to South America?" I try to sound casual. After all, we've only met a day ago. Or two, if the clock on the stove is correct.

"No, but I've always wanted to go. See the Andes, maybe Easter Island."

"And this project here? Can they keep doing it without you?"

"My sister would rather have me stay, but she'll find someone to replace me. And it's not forever."

Santiago would have been the last stop before Brazil, had I not been high on Xanax. I know how far away it is. We'll never see each other again.

"You can visit me."

The wine makes me a little dizzy.

"What's your book about?"

"The Mojave. It's a collection of photographs." He puts his fork down. "It's such a magical place, I can't even begin to describe it."

I remember the drive through the desert yesterday, and the sense of peace I felt in the hot spring at night.

"You don't have to go far, just half an hour east of here. There's Red Rock Canyon, and then going the other way, the Valley of Fire. I have to show you my favorite spots sometime."

He looks at me in a way that I'm not sure we're still talking about the desert. I should leave now. Get up, go to sleep.

Instead, I hear myself say, "I'd love to see your pictures."

"One's over there, in the hallway. And there's a black-and-white one in the living room."

He blows out the candle.

"But the best ones are in my room, for selected viewers only."

When he kisses me this time, I forget the plan to forget about him. My hands slide underneath his shirt. I want to touch every inch of his skin, I want to feel him inside me and stay in bed until the final call for his flight to Chile rings in my ears.

But then I pull away. Ben is not fling material. He is the one I'm in love with, and the one I'm in love with cannot live ten countries over. Eleven, I forgot El Salvador.

I'm curled up in one corner of the couch, closest to the fire. The flickering flames have calmed down and filled the room with a glow.

"And here are the dessert specials," he says, both hands behind his back. "Dark chocolate with cherries or almonds."

He holds up two unopened bars and sits beside me.

"Too many choices. I'll trust your judgment."

He feeds me a piece and I let the chocolate melt on my tongue.

"I didn't think it was possible, but your kiss tastes even more delicious now."

He moves away from my lips, down the side of my neck. Then he stops.

"Sorry, I promise I'll stay above your collarbone." He leans back and looks at me.

"Do you really need to leave, Paula?"

"My job, the bass, Max flying in. I'll have to."

"Tell him you met this guy in Vegas. Smart, sensitive, mad about you, he'll understand."

"He'll think I'm crazy."

"And what do you think, Paula?"

It's hard to think anything with him so close to me.

"I wouldn't know how to forget about you if we spent the night together."

"I don't want you to forget about me."

He leans on his elbow and looks into my eyes.

"Do you believe in love at first sight?"

I dig my fingernail into my thumb and let him kiss the pain away.

"I was in Canada as a kid," Ben says. My head lies on his chest and he plays with my hair.

"Really?"

"We lived in Detroit, and we'd cross the border for shopping. One summer my parents rented a cottage on the Canadian side. I liked it there."

The darkness, the wine, the incredibly long day, everything becomes blurred.

"Is your dad a teacher, too?" I ask, barely able to keep my eyes open.

"He's a physician. We moved there for his job, but my mother hated the weather in Michigan so much. I was fourteen when we came to Vegas."

"You have to see the west coast someday," I say with my eyes closed. "It's beautiful there."

"So, I've heard."

"I'm in heaven," I whisper. "How did I get here again?"

"You took a detour."

A whiff of foul breath wakes me up. I open one eye just enough to see Bear's gigantic head inches above mine. Ava was right about his drooling. I wipe my cheek and duck under the blanket, hoping he steps back a little.

"He likes you," Ben says. "Not everybody's this lucky."

Ben's eyes are half closed, and I admire his long lashes. Almost wasted on a man. If Bear isn't in Ava's room, it means that she's probably up.

"I should be going before everyone shows up for breakfast."

"So what? It's a commune."

"But I thought …"

"Okay, it's not. Still, look at you." He lifts up the blanket. "Not many Vegas tourists wake up fully dressed. Don't leave me alone with the smelly dog." Ben pulls me closer and I surrender to another wave of carefree sleep.

This time it's the smell of coffee that wakes me. The door to the kitchen is open and I see Ava. I put my feet down until I feel the wooden floor. Shoes in hand, I tiptoe through the room, quietly open the door, and sneak outside.

The sun must be about to come up, it's that moment between darkness and dawn when everything comes alive. It's got to be a good day when the birds are that cheerful.

The motorhome door is unlocked, and I make it onto my bed without waking Rita. It would be great to get some sleep, given that we'll be driving all through the night. But I'm wide awake, and the longer I lie here, the more restless I get. In my mind I replay every single touch, and all the things he said with so much tenderness. How did Rita put it the other day? I would know he's the one when the question doesn't even cross my mind. But my life's in Vancouver, not in the desert. It can't be Ben. At least now I know what it should feel like the next time I allow someone this close to my heart.

CHAPTER Twenty-six

I watch Rita pack her few belongings. She's moving into the guest room at Noah's Bark until her house on Seneca Drive is cleaned up.

"You must be happy to get home after all," she says.

"Yes." I chew on my lip. "It'll be good."

But the lightness I felt before is fading by the minute. Has it only been a week since I started this trip? I think back to Max talking me into this, and how I resisted. And then Rita, sweet, loving Rita. I want to pack her up and take her with me. Was it the same me who almost ditched her?

She folds her blanket with a smile. Rita seems to find joy, if not excitement in everything she does. I'm such a whiner compared to her. What do I have to complain about? Nothing bad has ever happened to me. I haven't lost a husband, or a baby. I've never risked anything. My life's as exciting as lukewarm coffee. A forgotten mug on the work desk, and I've been drinking out of it for so many years that I didn't even know there were options.

But now, during these past few days, a shot of espresso has messed with my senses and I don't know where I belong anymore. I've been telling myself that Jacobs Creek is behind me, but is it really? I didn't move to Australia when I should have, hiding instead behind the job and the apartment. Who was I fooling?

I watch Rita take her blouse off the hanger.

"About those parrots, what was it again that you read to me the other day?"

"This may be the moment to manifest your dreams," she says without looking up.

It sounds so right, and I wish I could start something new. Do I even know my dream? I have a list of things I don't want. I watch Rita feed Toto. Yesterday he was about to be abandoned, and now he lives with the kindest person in the world.

I will drive home tonight and figure out what my dream is. And I'll remember my weekend in Vegas like everybody else—a place where everything is possible until you wake up and it's Monday.

"Have I ever told you how I met my husband?" Rita pulls the zipper of her bag. "It was the day before the premiere of a new show at The Dunes. Our rehearsal pianist had slipped and broken a leg, so the director announced to the troupe that Mr. Valione would help us out. I didn't care one way or the other, since this casino gig was just a way to pay the bills until the audition for the San Francisco Ballet. So, we went through the whole program, and toward the end the girl next to me whispered that the new piano player was a lot younger and better-looking than Mr. Huckleton with his stringy combover. My view was covered by some props, so I had to take her word for it."

She picks up Toto and holds him on her lap.

"We happened to leave the building at the same time, Frank and I, and he held the door open for me. I can see it as if it were yesterday. He had raced in from a game of tennis, still in white shorts and all. The instant I looked at him, I knew. *Coup de foudre*, that's what the French call it. I literally felt that bolt of lightning. We stood there, talking, until he had to run to play at the Sands. 'Would you like to join me after the show?' he asked, and I did. That was 1966, and we never spent a day apart."

Toto lifts up his head and licks her hand.

"What I want to say is this. Sometimes you make plans and you think if you follow the script you'll be safe and comfortable. And this may be true for some people. But underneath all of that, there's a tiny bubble, smaller than a grain of rice. It never talks to you, it's just always there, like a quiet companion. That's the longing that moves you through life. The moment you meet your destiny, whether it's your talent, or a person, or even a place, the bubble expands. It fights for the right to be heard and doesn't care if you have other plans."

"My friend Max is flying here as we speak. He's doing all this to help me get back in time. I cannot let him down, I'm going home."

I get up and check the time.

"The comfort zone is a nice place to rest, but you shouldn't spend your life there," Rita says.

All of a sudden my body feels like lead. I can barely stand straight.

"Ben is moving to Chile. The-other-end-of-the-world Chile. And you know how these things go, at first you talk on the phone and you write each other, and then he'll meet someone, and then—"

My voice breaks and Rita puts her arm around me.

"You do what's best for you. Everything will be fine."

"I'll miss you."

"You know where to find me."

"Will you call me when you're settled in?" I scribble my number on a gas receipt. "Maybe I'll visit you."

She folds the piece of paper in her purse.

"I would love that."

Ben and I are on our way to the airport. We're in the vegan van, as Adam borrowed the other car and hasn't come back in time. Our last few hours together have flown by in a heartbeat. We've gone for a walk, we've talked, and when he went to fix the fence, I lay on a blanket in the sun watching him. And for the first time, I didn't worry about the future or regret the past. Which my friend back home calls the only way to deal with debt, climate change, and the remorse over her shaved head.

We're stopped behind a Super 8 courtesy shuttle when Max texts that they'll meet us outside.

"Gabe needs cigarette, c u," I read out loud. "I've never met the guy, but he annoys me already."

"We should be polite and let him finish his cigarette," Ben says and leans in for a kiss. Someone honks behind us and we move on to arrivals.

The designated smoking zone is a fenced-in concrete pad at the end of the taxi line, packed to capacity. At six foot three, Max sticks out from the crowd. I wave from the window, but he doesn't see me.

Ben double-parks and ignores the driver of a black Escalade who gives us the finger as he crawls by. It is definitely the most bejeweled middle finger I've ever been given. As I get out of the van, the Escalade's tinted windows slide down, releasing 150 decibels of subwoofed electro house.

"Move it bitch, this ain't hippie town," the driver yells and flicks a cigarette butt my way.

Adrenaline shoots through my body as I'm working on my counterattack.

"… the fuck you starin' at?" he says.

Obviously, my angry face doesn't impress him much. Just as my own middle finger unfolds and moves upward, Ben flies out of the van and bangs on the driver's side of the Escalade. After some shouting and door slamming the Escalade takes off, almost wiping out a Delta crew on the crosswalk.

I recognize Gabriel by his T-shirt. RELAX, The Drummer is Here. The letters are stretched tightly across his pumped pecs. A tall girl with a Panama hat laughs at something he says, and he lights her cigarette with the tip of his. Max talks to a pretty brunette.

"Hey guys, are you ready?"

Max hugs me and Gabriel pretends I don't exist.

"Could you maybe smoke a little faster? It's a no parking zone."

"Wow, you're fun," Gabriel says.

I can't stand him.

Max and I start walking toward the car.

"They're Dutch," he says. "Greta and Jannicke."

"So?"

"They loved our accent. Totally New York, they said. And they wanted to meet us for drinks."

"You're from Manitoba, Max."

"Potato Potahto."

"Besides, didn't you quit smoking last year?"

"Just chaperoning Don Juan here. Can't let him out of my sight for five minutes. The guy attracts trouble."

My thoughts circle back to Ben and how he was willing to take a fight for me. There could have been a gun or a knife, and yet—

"Hello, which way's the car?" Max snaps his fingers in front of my face. "Are you all right?"

"Uh-huh, yes. See the guy in the blue van over there? That's Ben."

"Ben? Is he the guy who puts this freakish smile on your face?"

"Maybe."

"I sense when a woman is sexually fulfilled. I'm quite perceptive that way."

"That's great, but there's nothing to perceive."

We're almost there, which cuts the investigation into my love life short. Ben jumps out as soon as he sees us, introduces himself and opens the hatch.

"I'll hold it up for you, the bar's broken," he says.

"Should I squeeze into the crate or hook up to the leash?" Gabriel asks.

"It's a short drive," Ben says. We both roll our eyes.

Gabriel crawls in first, then Max with his long legs. They sit sideways, leaning against their backpacks for comfort.

"Like we're in combat," Gabriel grunts.

"Yeah, remember that the next time you screw somebody's wife," Max says.

He picks a handful of fur off the floor and looks at Ben. "Are you a dog groomer or something?"

I still haven't seen the upper part of Gabriel's face. Maybe it rained in Vancouver, maybe he styles his hair like that, hard to say. It hangs flat over his eyes like a human-hair sleeping mask.

"The Dutch girls are staying at the D. She just texted me. Any chance we can stop there?" He shouts against the muffler noise.

Ben shrugs and switches to the right lane. "Fine with me."

"I don't know," Max says. "We have a long drive ahead of us, and the clock's ticking."

"One beer, man. You know the old saying, when in Rome—"

"—don't drink and ride the chariot?" Max says. "We're not here to party."

Gabriel doesn't give up easily. "Forget the beer then, let's hit a casino. Maybe they serve tea."

I feel his eyes stabbing me.

We park at the Golden Nugget and start walking along Fremont Street together. Gabriel is texting with the Panama hat and Max gets all excited about the SlotZilla Zip Line.

"Take a video, Paula," he shouts as he gets pushed ahead by the crowd.

Ben puts his arms around me from behind, and I feel like Kate Winslet on the Titanic. One hour is all we've got left. That's three thousand and six hundred seconds. Minus sixty for the video. Ben nibbles my ear and Max waves his arms at me from the platform. It could mean I'm next or I have to vomit. Either way I press the record button and follow someone in a blue harness screaming frantically above our heads.

"Sorry, we lost you guys somehow," Ben says when we all meet back at the van.

The truth is, we tried to walk to the landing pad, but somewhere between Binion's Gambling Hall and the world's largest fire hydrant, we got lost in the crowd and in each other's eyes.

"I can't believe I won." Max is beside himself. He fans the money like a deck of cards. "Twelve hundred dollars. I love you, Las Vegas."

Gabriel and his mop hair look unhappy. He's lost eighty bucks and hasn't found the Dutch sisters.

"Don't make such a face, dinner's on me." Max tries to cheer him up.

"Great. A drive-through in Fresno?"

"You can be a real pain sometimes. Are you even aware that we're doing all of this to save your ass?" Max explodes. "Paula's wasted a whole week, I'm paying for the flight, and all you do is bitch like the psycho Housewives of Orange County."

"Real," Gabriel says.

"What?"

"The Real Housewives of Orange County."

We're all squeezed into Adam's room, which seems to have gotten smaller since my last visit. Max looks at the wall of fame. He's completely ecstatic about the musicians in the pictures. "Herbie Hancock? You played with Herbie Hancock?"

"Yeah, a workshop at UCLA."

Gabriel drums on his knees with his eyes closed.

"My hero's Roy Haynes," he says. "Roy's like, God, only better, you know what I mean?"

"Sure do." Adam plucks the same string on the bass over and over.

"I hate to spoil the moment, but we should get on our way," Max says.

Adam starts wrapping the canvas around the instrument. "You can send this baby down anytime," he says to me. "I know guys who'd kill for a Prescott."

"Me too," Gabriel says.

"She's in great shape, respect. Apart from the little crack."

Gabriel stops drumming. "A crack, like, in the body?"

"Yep. Take a look, right here."

"It's new." Gabriel parts his hair to see better. "It wasn't there when I got it."

Gabriel looks at me as if everything were my fault.

"Well, it's really small." Max clears his throat. "And obviously you can still play it."

"Sure. Except that you're driving back through the same weather conditions," Adam says. "It might expand."

Gabriel jumps up. "I'm not taking it anywhere with a crack. This lawyer guy is crazy." He taps his fingers against his forehead.

"What do you want to do, hide in Vegas for the rest of your life?" Max is getting louder.

"At least hang low for a while." Gabriel stands up and puts both hands on his hips.

"Have you lost it now? You got us into all this shit!"

Max towers over him by a foot.

"The guy knows some scary dudes, I'd rather feed the birds at the Flamingo."

"You'll start gigging here in no time," Adam says. "Just get your name out and stuff, you know how it works."

"Sure," Max says. "Everyone's just waiting for an asshole drummer without drums."

He kicks the coffee table.

"Dude, you've got to relax." Gabriel takes out his phone and starts scrolling. "There, five hundred bucks for a Mapex kit. How far is Henderson?"

"Ten miles," Adam says. "I can take you there."

"Cool, thanks man." He holds up his hand for a high five.

"That's it?" Max yells. "You're really doing this?"

"You gotta understand, man, I can't show up with a broken bass."

"So, my ass gets kicked instead?"

"You'll be fine, he only hates *me*."

"That makes two," Max says.

He's clenching his fist and takes a step toward Gabriel. Then he exhales and punches the wall.

"Do me a favor, Gabriel. Get the fuck out of my life. Don't ever call me again. Not a text, not a word. Ever."

"Not even if Cirque du Soleil needs a piano player?"

"Not even if Miles fucking Davis comes back from the dead and wants me for his world tour."

"Got it, no tour with Miles."

Max picks up the bass and storms out of the room. "Shithead."

I hug Adam, ignore Gabriel, and run to find Max. He's on the gravel path to the parking lot when I catch up with him. His face is red and he's grinding his teeth.

"You're the only reliable friend I have," he says. "When you say something, you stick with it. I like that."

"Didn't you call me 'rigid and boring' last week?"

"No, I said, you need a little adventure." His voice softens. "Judging by your dreamy eyes I'd say, mission accomplished. You're welcome."

CHAPTER Twenty-seven

"**I'm not good** with goodbyes," Ben says. "Promise that we'll see each other again."

"I promise."

Our arms are wrapped around one another and I don't want to let go.

"I hate to interrupt, but we should get on our way," Max says.

I look at the Winnebago and understand what my father sees in it. "All I love in this world is in here. What else do I need?" He used to say those exact words on our summer trips.

He's right, life can be wonderful within twenty-two feet.

"Here's something for the road." Ava hands me a paper bag.

"It was great meeting you, Paula. Take care."

"Thanks, Ava. Thank you for everything."

We hug, then I pet Bear who sticks to her like a shadow.

"Hey Max, have you met Ben's sister?"

He's about to disappear into the motorhome.

"This is my friend Max, the guy who sent me here."

He turns around and freezes. He opens his mouth to speak but doesn't say anything.

"Nice to meet you," Ava says.

Max nods in silence. Not a quick nice-to-meet-you-nod, but the silly-looking kind that goes on and on. I've never seen him shy around women.

He needs to wake up from lalaland. I tap his shoulder.

"Ready to go, Max?"

He looks at me, then at Ava, confused.

"That's a big dog you've got." He reaches out to pet Bear.

"He's a St. Bernard," she says.

"St. Bernard. They used to live with Swiss monks, right? For search and rescue in the mountains I believe."

"That's right. I'm impressed."

"And they always had a small brandy barrel around the neck."

His eyes avoid Ava. He pets the dog until his hand is covered in slobber.

"That's a myth," Ava says.

"Really? It must be quite the persistent myth then. Maybe the monks drank it themselves."

He dries his hand on his jeans.

"It's because of a painting," Ava says. "Some artist, for whatever reason, portrayed a mountain dog with a keg around his neck. And that was two hundred years ago, but it stuck."

"Huh. I didn't know that."

"Do you have a dog?"

"No, I don't. Not at the moment."

He shoots a glance at her and attempts a smile.

"My mother has a dog, though. George. He's a poodle."

I turn away as I can't keep a straight face. His mother's poodle? I'm clearly not the only one whose brain shuts down around the Barlow family.

"Anyway, I'm afraid we need to leave. But when I do need a dog, I know where to find one."

"Great," Ava says. "Maybe you'll both come down next time."

"That would be—yes, definitely, we'll do that."

I leave Max and his primeval babbling and go look for Rita. She is sitting on a bench in the shade and gets up when she sees me.

"Take care, sweetie," she says.

"Who's going to teach me all about life?"

"You won't need it anymore." She takes my hand in hers.

"I'll miss you, Rita. And I can't believe I'm saying this, but meeting you has been the best thing in my life."

"It's only the beginning, you'll see."

We hug until I turn away to blow my nose.

I walk over to Max and Ben who shake hands and slap each other's back, bro-hug light.

"Hey you." Ben puts his arm around me.

"I'll give you three minutes, then I'll honk," Max says and disappears inside.

Ben turns to face me and wipes a tear off my cheek.

"Take good care of Luna, please."

Before I get to finish, Ben's lips are on mine. His body's so close that I feel his heartbeat. His kiss tells me everything words can't say. It is tender and passionate at once, like every moment we've shared.

"Tick tock." Max knocks against the windshield and points at his wrist. I run my hand through Ben's hair for the last time.

A framed postcard on Valentina's desk comes to my mind. It looks like a child's drawing of a fox, and it says, "You become responsible, forever, for what you have tamed." She told me that Philip gave it to her when they got engaged, and that it's a quote from *The Little Prince.* I finally understand.

"By the way," Ben says. "We've found a home for her."

"Sorry, what?"

"Luna, she'll be adopted."

"But you said it'll take a while for an older dog like her. Are they good people?"

The lump in my throat is getting bigger. I was secretly hoping she'd stay here.

"It's me." Ben strokes my face with the back of his hand. "Every time I see her, I think of you, and I want to keep it that way."

"That's … the sweetest thing ever."

"I thought that was me bringing you croissants on Saturdays," Max shouts from behind the wheel and starts the engine.

I look out the window until the lights of Noah's Bark disappear. Max has offered to do the first shift of driving. He's checked the weather forecast and decided to take the long way home. Too much snow in the interior. I'm in the passenger seat with the map spread out and we're turning south onto the I-15.

"Please tell me I didn't really say those things out loud," Max says. "It was only in my head, right?"

"Straight out of your big mouth. Is that your new move?"

He bangs his fist on the steering wheel. "This woman is a goddess and I'm a total idiot. How bad was it?"

"Well, you got pretty hung up on the whole barrel thing."

"Fuck."

"The poodle story didn't help."

He's shaking his head.

"At least I didn't tell her why he's called George."

"Can you tell *me*?"

"Colin Firth."

"I don't get it."

"My mom's completely hung up on Colin Firth, and he played King George in *The King's Speech*."

"Better you skipped that."

"Yeah."

The city limits are behind us and we're driving farther into the desert.

"Would you date me after that, if you didn't know I was such a cool cat?"

"Nah."

"Really?"

"Kidding. Of course, I'd go out with you, and so would Ava."

Max is smiling to himself.

"She's unreal."

"I know."

"Does she have a boyfriend?"

"No."

He starts to hum.

"Of course, there's this thing."

"What thing?" The humming stops.

"She's vegan."

"That's it?" He sounds relieved. "You had me scared here for a moment. Vegan's fine with me."

"How generous of you to say that, but you don't understand. *She* wouldn't be with *you*. You'd have to convert."

"I could do that."

It sounds more like a question.

"No leather, no honey, no chocolate, unless it's something like 200% cacao. She dumped the last guy because he wouldn't help her release piglets from a trailer."

"As in, mobile home?"

"No, as in trailer truck. On the way to the slaughterhouse."

"Eww."

"It was stopped with a flat tire, and Ava wanted to get the piglets out while the driver was busy, but her boyfriend refused. I don't know all the details."

"But she's so angelic."

"She left the boyfriend by the side of the road."

"Hmm."

"So, would you?" I ask him.

"Would I what?"

"Give up meat for love?"

"If someone like Ava wanted to date me, I'd personally flatten the tires of a slaughterhouse truck."

He accelerates to pass an eighteen-wheeler.

"At least she's not crazy enough to drive a car with all those stickers plastered on it, like your lover."

"It's hers, Max."

CHAPTER Twenty-eight

We're crossing the California state line.

"What did Lamar say when you told him he's not getting the bass?"

"I never told him," Max says.

"Maybe you should."

"I don't want to be in his bad books."

"I see. And while he sits in Malibu, waiting for the bass that'll never arrive, you'll be in his good books?"

"Maybe not good per se. But zero karma. One of those, hey-tha t-nice-Canadian-guy-never-showed-up-but-he-refunded-my-money kind of book."

"They don't exist."

"Sure they do, it's Buddhism."

"Huh?"

Max opens a bag of barbecue potato chips with his teeth.

"Want some?"

"No thanks. But I want to hear that philosophical angle."

"It's all about detachment." He shoves a handful of chips in his mouth. "Lamar wants the bass, but he doesn't get it. The lesson is, you can't control life."

"Buddha said that?"

"Basically, yeah."

"You made all that up because you're afraid to call him?"

He swipes the greasy crumbs from his lap.

"I'm Zen."

"You're crazy."

He rolls his eyes at me.

"Hey Paula, speaking of unfinished business, aren't we going to your ex's party next weekend?"

I haven't thought of Julian all day.

"Do I still play your boyfriend when we see him?"

"Thanks. Not necessary anymore."

"Too bad. I enjoyed our fake make-out."

Max opens a can of Coke and drinks it in one go.

"Don't you want to fill me in?" he says. "Your life has taken up some speed since I've last seen you. Tell me about the web of passion and betrayal, love lost, love found."

"It's not a soap opera."

"Okay, fill me in on the ordinary existence of Paula M. But spice it up a bit, I need to stay awake."

"There'll be no party, and the wedding is off."

"What? Does that mean your ex is free again, ready for sexy little Paula to make her move?"

"Sexy little Paula doesn't need to do anything. He wants me back as I am."

"Great. It's what you wanted, right?"

"Last Sunday, yes."

"And today?"

He glances at me.

"I don't know, things happened."

A highway patrol car races past us, emergency lights flashing.

"Maybe I can help you with the male perspective. Go on, I'm a good listener."

I pull my knees up to my chest and look out into the dark. The last exit for a town was miles ago. It'll be nothing but desert until we hit the big Interstate Highway.

"Would you mind turning up the heat?"

He sets the control button to five. "Here, take this."

He steers the RV with one hand at a time while he takes off his hoodie.

"Thanks, Max."

"No worries." He runs his hand through his hair. "Now, back to your love life."

"Do you remember when you were young and thought that peaches were the most delicious fruit in the world, and then you had your first mango?"

"I'm allergic to mangos," Max says.

"How can you be allergic to mangos?"

"I get sneezing fits."

"Anyway. I used to think we only had one shot at true love, and that Julian was the one for me. And when he was gone, I felt anyone else could only be second best. But then I met Ben, and the way I feel about him—there are no words really. And then Julian calls off the wedding."

"The peach?"

"Exactly. But the mango, I don't even know where to start. It's sweet, it's tasty, it's perfect. All I want to have is mango, but Canada's not a tropical place. Unfortunately."

"So, the peach's back on the table?"

"No. Are you not listening?"

"Hey, interesting fact—too many mangos can cause diarrhea. I just read it in the inflight magazine on the way down."

"Seriously, are we still talking about the same thing?"

"I think it's the fiber."

I doubt Max is the right person for relationship advice.

"There is no problem," he says. "You're coming home, your ex is there, life is good."

"That's … very pragmatic."

"The things you want only happen in movies."

"Hmm."

"Anything else I can do for you?"

I wish I could see the world through his eyes for just one day. We pass a road sign. Five hundred miles to Sacramento. I don't want to talk anymore.

"Sometimes life sucks," Max says after a while.

"Big time."

"I don't know how Buddha did it."

"You're the expert."

He sighs.

"I don't have a clue, Paula. I just make shit up as I go. They should teach relationship stuff in school. Who cares about the seventh root of eight, or which king stole what from whom?"

"You're supposed to cheer me up here."

"If you don't want to be with Julian, then don't. I didn't like the guy anyway."

"Anything in particular?"

"I don't know. His voice. The way he treated you. And that you felt the need to lie."

"That's on me."

"Still. You deserve better."

He pushes the radio button. Snowstorm on the east coast. Monsanto loses a lawsuit. President pardons Thanksgiving turkey. White noise, then nothing.

"Could you find some music, please."

"Carpenters or Elton John?" I hold up both tapes for him to choose.

"Surprise me."

We've been driving for three hours or so when Max pulls into the parking lot of a Carl's Junior.

"We need gas, but I need to fill up first," he says as we walk inside. "Dinner's on me, go wild."

I order a chicken club and a garden salad.

"Jalapeño cheeseburger with fries for me," Max says.

He heads for the washroom and I load up on ketchup at the condiment station. Then we both stop and look at each other.

"Are you thinking the same?" he asks.

I nod.

The tired-looking kid behind the counter lowers a deep fryer into the sizzling oil.

"Excuse me," Max says. "I'd like to change our order."

The boy punches something into the till.

"No meat. We'll have two veggie burgers instead."

"That'll be five minutes."

"Thanks."

"For the animals. Slaughterhouses and stuff, you know?"

"Sure."

Max puts two quarters in the tip jar.

"Would you like bacon on the salad?"

"I can drive for a while."

"I'm good, thanks," Max says. "Get some rest. We're pulling an all-nighter."

I recline against the backrest and stretch out my legs. The strip mall is brightly lit, and we wobble over a few speed bumps before the ride is smooth again.

The more I try to relax, the more awake I feel. Images come up, like thumbnails on a screen. Ben's eyes when we said goodbye, the night he cooked for me, Cinderella and the lentils, Christmas lights at the language school, Luna.

"I can't sleep. How much time have we made, an hour?"

"Seven minutes."

Max tries the radio again, and this time it stays on.

"Soft jazz, is that okay with you?"

I close my eyes.

"We should be happier by now."

"Silje Nergaard, I love this woman."

Max turns up the volume.

"Is she from Iceland, too?"

"Norway."

The song is beautiful, just like her voice. It tells the story of a lover left behind and how it should feel right but it doesn't. I shiver at her words. This Norwegian woman who's never met me knows exactly what I want. The highway sign, Exit 179 Bakersfield, does not. It's the one that sends us north, and north is wrong.

I straighten up in my seat.

"Turn around," I say as the highway's about to split.

"Have you lost it?" Max asks and stays in the lane for Bakersfield.

"Turn this thing around, I'm not going back."

"You can't do this."

"Max, please."

He hits the brakes hard and we come to a stop on the shoulder.

"This is not a romantic comedy, Paula. If we turn around now, that's it. You'll lose your job, you won't be able to pay the rent, it's all over."

A passing driver honks his horn at us.

"Nothing's over, this is a beginning. My friend Rita told me about the rice bubble and I'm feeling it."

"Has everyone gone crazy today?"

"Don't you see? This is what you've been telling me all along. Be fearless, don't overthink, be free."

"And you're absolutely sure that's what you want?"

"Positive." I'm bursting inside.

Max curses as he gets back on the overpass and accelerates into the southbound lane.

"Thank you, Max. Love you forever."

"I love you, too."

One hour before we reach Vegas, Max is done being mad at me. I haven't stopped talking since we turned around and he knows everything that's happened on this crazy trip.

"I still wish you'd come back with me, but I understand."

I unbuckle and lean over for a quick kiss on his cheek.

"I've got to tell you something," he says when I'm back in my seat. "Maybe it's Las Vegas, or maybe we're all nuts. But when I was out casino hopping with Gabriel and won all that money, I thought, what if I took the bass to Lamar after all? I mean, shit, it's Lamar. This is probably the only chance I'll get in my life. Even while I had my lucky streak, and some beautiful girls were talking to us, all I could think of was how much I wanted to go to L.A. and see what happens. Am I crazy?"

"You're not crazy. It's your bubble."

"I have no idea what you're talking about."

"Somehow it made more sense when Rita explained it. But you should go, Max. Take the Winnebago."

"Seriously?"

"It's insured till March. Do it."

"What about your dad?"

"I'll talk to him."

His face is lit by the oncoming traffic. He's smiling to himself.

"I can get a keyboard, hang out a bit, camp along the Pacific Highway on my way home."

"Do you have concerts coming up?"

"Regular Christmas stuff. Anybody can play that."

"Does the scary lawyer know your name?"

"Nope, it all went through Gabe. Wife sold it to him, he sold it to me. Everything in cash, plus everyone had fun for a while. Not my problem if she goes back to the rich fart. Apparently, he's constantly cheating on her."

"Why'd she go back then?"

"At first it was exciting to run off with a musician. But she didn't like the furniture at their rental, her credit card was cancelled, and there were no malls. And she really hated Newfoundland because of her implants."

"What?"

"The temperature. St. John's has been unusually cold. Turned them into snowballs as soon as she went outside."

My life feels so normal.

"Anyway, her husband promised her a new Hummer if she came back. A Hummer for a drummer."

"Max, you're doing the right thing."

"Exactly. Why should Lamar be punished for an early winter on the East Coast?"

We're back in Vegas at three in the morning. Max parks the RV down the road so the dogs won't bark. I stuff everything into my backpack as fast as I can.

"If it doesn't work out with mango man, I want you back," Max says.

He unlocks the door and I hug him.

"Thanks for kicking me out of the nest last week."

"You were ready to fly."

He gets behind the wheel and drives into the dark. Maybe all those dreams my father put in the Winnebago years ago have turned it into a magic carpet. An owl hoots from the nearby tree as I walk toward the house. I catch a last glimpse of the taillights, and I picture Max meeting Lamar, his hero, the two of them playing together at the beach house. Max may not know it, but he's in for a ride.

Rita is in the bedroom facing the parking lot. I knock on her window.

"Now *you* surprise me," she says as she lets me in.

"I'll tell you everything tomorrow."

We hug and I sneak into the hallway. My heartbeat is louder than the knock on Ben's door. I wait, then knock again. He opens the door and rubs his eyes.

"Am I dreaming?"

He pulls me inside, his smile widening. I kick off my shoes and let my coat slide to the ground.

"I haven't seen the Valley of Fire yet."

Acknowledgments

Thank you to the gentleman in the sweater vest who interviewed me for the weekend relief position at a local seniors home. Apparently I was not qualified to answer the phone and show residents to the dining hall. So I stopped reaching for the stars and became a novelist. I'm planning to forgive him someday. Or I'll buy the place and have him transferred to housekeeping.

I would also like to thank everybody who really helped me:

Jonas Saul, my excellent editor, for keeping me on track and for making me get back to work each time I thought I was done.

My writer friends AK White, J.C. Corry, and Jenn Marx. You guys have been the icing on the cake of the Surrey International Writers' Conference.

The Surrey International Writers' Conference for being the icing on the cake of conferences.

Wendy McAlpine for putting me at ease while taking the author portraits, and for all the laughs we shared before, during, and after. Cheers, Wendy.

Silje Nergaard for her soulful music. Without "We Should be Happier by Now," Paula may not have turned around.

Thank you *Schitt's Creek* and Netflix for making me laugh no matter what.

Andrea Giesen for dragging me to each and every creative writing class there was, no matter how far the drive, how bad the weather, or how pregnant we were. Also, for being the friend you can call at three in the morning.

Stephen, Simon, and Alex, my beta readers and so much more. Thank you for your love and support, for accepting that I'm not a morning person, and for giving me sugar-free, honest feedback even when I don't want to hear it. Also, thank you for letting me sing in your band sometimes.

And finally, I did have a rescue dog named Luna. She'd been abused and left to die, chained to an abandoned shed.

This book is for Luna and all the dogs out there who're just waiting for their lives to begin.

Made in the USA
Middletown, DE
17 July 2021

44113367R00135